Praise for *The Dance and the Fire*

Los Angeles Times, A Best Book of Summer
W Magazine, A Best Book of Summer

"A kaleidoscopic, erudite, and sweepingly tender novel reminiscent of Sebald, if Sebald were on acid. *The Dance and the Fire*'s power comes from the ambitious (yet brilliantly compacted) range of its themes—fatherhood, eros, art, judgment, personal and archival aporia—that culminate in a book as capacious, porous, and resonant as history itself."

—Ocean Vuong, author of *On Earth We're Briefly Gorgeous*

"Daniel Saldaña París's new novel, *The Dance and the Fire*, has everything a reader could want: climate dystopia, hysterical dancing, and a long-standing love triangle . . . As the surrounding landscape succumbs, one friend seeks solace in dance. Inspired by German Expressionism and medieval danse macabre, the performance expands into something more intense than any of them anticipated, fracturing boundaries between the present world and the past, between myth and reality."

—Isle McElroy, *Vulture*

"Saldaña París' reconstruction of this centuries-old tale feels vibrant and urgent in this age of wildfires and pandemics."

—Alejandra Oliva, *Americas Quarterly*

"The fires provide both a backdrop and a running metaphor. Saldaña París is interested in inflammation and contagion—as in searing pain, easy gossip, sleazy pastors, catching conspiracy, smoldering desire."

—Meghan Racklin, *The Brooklyn Rail*

"*The Dance and the Fire*'s achievement is in giving the story of a friendship such depth and difficulty that it holds its own against the absurd events of the novel's third act. In the end, the novel's commitment to the 'dense undergrowth' behind the mundane details of relation allows it to operate in simultaneously tragic and comic registers. Its tripartite interiority balances the bleak visuals of the burning city."

—Molly MacVeagh, *World Literature Today*

"A sophisticated tour-de-force centering the ungovernable forces that nourish, propel, and destroy us. Saldaña París's cerebral, compassionate prose encompasses a vast range of lived experiences, including the domestic, the uncanny, and the beautifully flawed." —Sofija Popovska, *Asymptote Journal*

"*The Dance and the Fire* brought Saldaña París as much insight into the secrets of his character(s) as it brought me into the search so many of us undertake for the fundamental details of our own stories, details that have been simply misplaced or even buried under the ashes of the past."

—Cory Oldweiller, *Southwest Review of Books*

"In telling *The Dance and the Fire* through three voices, the story comes at us in compelling bits and pieces defined by the often-pinhole perspectives of each. The stakes, too, are there in the background of these personal dramas—the city seemingly on the brink of explosion, its inextinguishable fires a dread-inducing bass line that won't let up."

—Diana Arterian, *Literary Hub*

"*The Dance and the Fire* is an evocative portrait of sexuality, friendship, and art, amongst a setting of nearby destruction."

—Sam Franzini, *Our Culture*

"With *The Dance and the Fire*, Saldaña París takes experimental leaps—juxtaposing voices, tones, and literary styles . . . It's a heady novel of relationships and ideas that has not left me in the months since I first read it."

—Willem Marx, *Electric Literature*

"A smoldering tale of three friends whose erotic and artistic dynamics rouse a Mexican city from its collective slumber."

—Sophia Stewart, *The Millions*

"*The Dance and the Fire* is exuberantly strange, dark, and comic: an enthralling ode to Cuernavaca and the modern rebirth of medieval choreomania, as well as a prophecy about what happens when the built-up dread of our world on fire begins to seep into the soul. Daniel Saldaña París is an extraordinary talent, and his novel feels both urgent and true."

—Lauren Groff, author of *Fates and Furies*

"Saldaña París's prose is subtle, and his intelligence diaphanous. But be aware: the characters and the stories that bring them together are ferocious." —Álvaro Enrigue, author of *You Dreamed of Empires*

"An absorbing and alarming chimera of a novel in which past meets present, fantasy meets flesh, and individual malaise collides with the woes of a vast and unraveling society. Saldaña París is a deft and clever storyteller."

—C. Pam Zhang, author of *Land of Milk and Honey*

"*The Dance and the Fire* is a wonder, brimming with hypnotic prose, wildly vivid descriptions, and intimately—and intricately—drawn characters. It's as explosive as wildfire, yet as precise and graceful as meticulously crafted choreography. All that remains is to dance."

—Isaac Fitzgerald, author of *Dirtbag, Massachusetts*

The Dance and the Fire

ALSO BY DANIEL SALDAÑA PARÍS

Among Strange Victims
Ramifications
Planes Flying over a Monster

The Dance and the Fire

A Novel

Daniel Saldaña París

TRANSLATED FROM THE SPANISH
BY CHRISTINA MACSWEENEY

Catapult
New York

THE DANCE AND THE FIRE

This is a work of fiction. All of the characters, organizations, and events portrayed in this novel are either products of the author's imagination or used fictitiously.

First Catapult edition: 2025
First paperback edition: 2026

Hardcover ISBN: 978-1-64622-245-2
Paperback ISBN: 978-1-64622-332-9

Library of Congress Control Number: 2024951094

Cover design by Farjana Yasmin
Cover image © iStock / darkbird77
Book design by Wah-Ming Chang

Catapult
New York, NY
books.catapult.co

Printed in the United States of America

10 9 8 7 6 5 4 3 2 1

Revolution rages too in the tierra caliente *of each human soul.*

MALCOLM LOWRY

Contents

The Great Noise 1

A Clear-Cut Vision 91

Bioluminescent Beach 175

Acknowledgments 239

The Great Noise

I watered the bromeliads a while ago, when the chill morning wind from the mountains was still blowing through the neighborhood, one of the highest in Cuernavaca. The bromeliads are beautiful, but something more too. If that's all they were, I wouldn't shower so much attention on them: beauty is repose, or at least a form of stability, of balance, but with the bromeliads, I can sometimes discern a hint or forewarning of disorder, the imminence of disaster; it's as if they are always on the verge of changing. There's an uneasy tension about them, like mountain goats with their hooves perched on the edge of a precipice. Some bromeliads look like monsters; delicate dragons, carnal, carnivorous, animal flowers. Counting the one I found in the forest not so long ago, I now have a dozen different varieties. That's not many; I'd like to have an example of each of the three thousand or so species in existence; to collect them the way you do coins or stamps. I imagine them on an endless terrace with red clay tiles, spaced out at the regulation distance. Soldiers in an implausible, extraterrestrial army; dancers in a ballet company composed of three thousand soloists, standing poised in the spotlights—the two suns of their strange planet—awaiting a signal from me to move.

I discovered the last one lying on a path, as though it were waiting for me there. I sometimes imagine things that way: that plants are waiting for me, that they are destined for me in some dark, subterranean way I can't quite figure out. (In general, the world seems like a system of allusions and signs, like Baudelaire's forest of symbols but with treeless areas; a Morse code of objects and people that is only partly legible; a book chewed to shreds by a furious dog.) The trunk that the roots of the bromeliad were attached to had snapped, maybe because the trees are getting too little water, far too little water. I rap on some of the trunks, like knocking on a door, and they seem almost hollow: the carcasses of trees erected on a stage, waiting for the entrance of the lead character: fire. There's been no rain for several months; wildfires have been spreading throughout the state like an insidious rumor, decimating the woodland. Argoitia warned me that right now isn't a good time to go hiking in the forest; fire might be lying in wait for me at a turn of the path, like the wolf in "Little Red Riding Hood." But I'm less afraid of it than of men, and since the wildfires began, I haven't met a single person during my walks. But I do have to tie a scarf around the lower part of my face—as though I were crossing the Sahara—to prevent the invisible ash entering my lungs and lodging there.

The bromeliad on the path in El Tepeite—the hillside not far from the house—is less monstrous than the others, it has an air of fragility. It's a *Tillandsia*, commonly known as the "carnation of the air." I recognized the genus almost immediately, because it's native to this part of the world, but I still checked it out on the internet when I got home to confirm my conjecture. I'd never pull a bromeliad from its branch, but this one, having fallen onto the path, asphyxiated by the drought, like a fish out of water, was begging me to pick it up. Its leaves are so long and fine they almost seem like stamens; the plants' extremities. They—*Tillandsia*—are like restless fairies. Bats pollinate them with a kiss, and there is, in fact, something bat-like about them: the one I found is dark, the color of certain two-day-old bruises. When I picked it up and brought it home, I felt like I was rescuing a young bird that had fallen from its nest. It seemed exhausted. It had probably been asphyxiated by the smoke from the fires, was suffering from lack of rainwater and the rising temperatures of the endless summer that is desiccating the whole region. I'd almost swear that the *Tillandsia* was having palpitations—rapid, headlong palpitations, close to giving up—but it was more likely my heart that was pounding, the blood beating in the arteries of my wrists. I used wire to attach my chance find to a piece of the decomposing eucalyptus that Argoitia had had dumped at the far end of the garden—a half-wild area where we've allowed the weeds to flourish—and that I had relocated to the terrace. That way, it will be able to wheedle its roots into the dead tree. I wonder if it would do the same in my head. I could fix the *Tillandsia* there with wire, like one of those exotic sunhats women used to wear in the 1920s, so the plant could sink its roots between the sutures of my skull, separating the frontal and parietal bones like someone digging their fingers into sand, until my skull was fully open and it could drink the liquid in which my brain floats, until it knew everything I know—and would one day like to forget—and think about the things I think of, the things I can't stop thinking of.

My twelve bromeliads are arranged along the length of an adobe wall—together with stone, adobe is the main material used in the construction of this house. Some hang from trunks while others, the ones requiring soil, are planted in pots at the foot of the wall. I use a mister to water them, as if I were going to style their hair afterward. I never had dolls as a child but imagine that my friends used to play with theirs that way. The difference is that my dolls are alive. I sometimes feel they are stretching, that the water wakes them and they slowly stretch out to the light filtering through the branches of the avocado tree.

I'm tired. I slept badly: it was one of those nights when I tossed and turned and then woke feeling all hot and guilty, like I'd committed incest or broken a Greek amphora in my sleep.

Argoitia wants me to accompany him to a lunch at Las Mañanitas, where the other guests will be insufferable people of his generation and circle—male writers in ties who like to be called "sir," ladies who wear pantyhose despite the awful heat, politicians who keep pet zebras—but I'm going to say I can't go, that I have work to do here in the study.

This morning, when he asked me, I didn't give a straight

answer. When I say, "this morning," it was in fact already past midday: Argoitia gets up at noon or one. He has breakfast at the wrought-iron table on the terrace, unless the wind has blown from the east of the city during the night, bringing with it smoke and ash. There are clear signs of rust beneath the flaked white paint of the table and the heavy chairs, but Argoitia insists on leaving them that way and having breakfast outdoors whenever possible. I sometimes spy on him from the study; he looks fragile, bewildered, wrapped in his cotton bathrobe, a plate of fruit before him, fat and badly shaved, his thinning hair uncombed and too long at the back. Before donning his lynx expression, before drinking his coffee and regaining the conviction that he deserves everything he has—this adobe-and-stone house, the garden, his position as permanent consultant to the Ministry of Culture, the Carlos Mérida painting in the living room—Argoitia is a sad, aging man who silently eats fruit and listens to the birdsong. That's when I start to find him attractive all over again.

From around seven in the morning—when I usually wake—to noon, I have the house to myself. It's the only period when I feel completely comfortable within these walls. I water the bromeliads with the mister, put food out for the cat, and sometimes read. I do very little work during that time; instead, I tend to just be there, occupying the space. Then, when Argoitia wakes, I shut myself in the study to work, to do everything I didn't do the whole morning.

It's not so much that I'm avoiding Argoitia, I just prefer to use my solitude to do nothing, to sit in this armchair and observe the long wall of bromeliads. During my working hours,

I read books and make notes, watch videos on the internet and make notes, flip through art catalogues and make notes. That's all I do, and at the moment no one is paying me to do it.

I sometimes think moving in with Argoitia was a mistake. In a kind of pained stupor, I think of the women who lived here before me, who slept in the bed I sleep in and ate at the table I eat at, who tried to persuade him—unsuccessfully—to paint the wrought-iron chairs in the garden, who stroked the cat I stroke with the same combination of affection and respect, wary of being scratched. For Argoitia, as well as for the cat, there's a continuity: a series of replaceable women, passing one after the other more or less naturally—a succession of almost identical, respectful strokings, silences, noises, and smells—like when I was a girl and my dog died or went missing and my mom would bring me another that she'd rescued from the streets of Tepoztlán or was given by a neighbor.

One of those dogs, Capone, bit my calf one evening. Capone was a mid-size dog with a reddish coat, not unlike a fox in appearance. Mom had found him tied up with a cable near a soccer pitch and had set him free; Capone followed her home across the whole town. Thunderclaps used to drive him crazy, as if they were reminders of some partially repressed past. The moment a storm broke, the dog would start running around the house, toppling everything in his path, his tongue hanging out and his eyes bulging. After a while he'd crouch under the table and stay there motionless, whining in anguish.

But that evening, he didn't stay there quietly. There was a particularly heavy storm, the sort we haven't experienced for a long time. Capone broke a terra-cotta plant pot and when I tried to pat his coat to calm him, he bit me. It was a serious bite, not just a scratch. I remember being surprised that my blood was so dark, as thick as the resin that flows from pine branches on campfires.

I still have the scar: a plump, twisty worm that rounds my ankle and ascends my calf. The skin of the scar is pinker and more sensitive than the soft surrounding flesh, and I can't bear anyone to touch it. For years I was even embarrassed about it being seen; I hid it from lovers and strangers alike, took to wearing pants and knee-high boots, even on the hottest days.

When Capone bit me, my mother took me to the community health center, but there were no doctors on duty so a nurse had to do the stitches; I guess it must have been her first time, and maybe her last. Mom made me look away, but at some point I turned my head. What is stamped on my memory isn't the suture, but the expression of the nurse's face as she sewed: a look of concentration that could also have been panic. I owe the worm on my lower leg to that anonymous and possibly poorly qualified woman. And to Capone, of course; my mom wanted to have him put down the next day, but the dog's pleading eyes were too much for the veterinarian and he adopted Capone. A few months later, during another storm, Capone also attacked his savior and that's when his luck ran out. But I know now that it wasn't Capone's fault. Whichever way you look at it, the culprit was the imbecile who had systematically mistreated him, tied him up with a cable and left him there in the rainy season until Mom gave him a home.

Naturally, Capone is the dog I remember best. The others form a list of indistinguishable pets (Pontífice, Basura, Vlady . . .) who spent a while with us before joining one of the packs of strays that roamed the town, fed by everyone but answering to no one—free and feral, as dogs ought to be, revered and feared by the townsfolk, spoiled by butchers; a howling mob that used to raise the bristles of the night.

I always remember negative things more clearly: the day my mom forgot to pick me up from school glows in my memory with an intensity that eclipses the many years she turned up punctually. The same goes for Capone: on the rare occasions when we have a storm sufficiently heavy to evoke my childhood ones, I recall his spastic movements, his bulging eyes, the white slaver drooling from his mouth, and then, with a fingertip moistened with saliva, I stroke the scar on my calf.

With Argoitia, I'm going to be the dog that bites, even if that bite takes the twisted form of all human things. I'm not going to be replaced by some student of his ten years younger than me, because I'm going to leave him without so much as a word before that happens, and he'll never ever forget me, just like in a ranchera song. He'll have a photo of me in his wallet the day he falls victim to a heart attack or respiratory failure under the brownish skies of the forest fires, in the courtyard of the Centro Morelense de las Artes, watched with astonishment by a score of people (pale secretaries, visibly moved drama students, dumbstruck parents). They'll call me from the hospital because I'll still be listed as his emergency contact, and I'll quite simply say nothing, listening to the perplexed voice of the nurse, with the ECG beeping too slowly, too weakly in the background. That's a fantasy I return to from time to time with a sort of morbid pleasure. Not from malevolence or cunning, I just enjoy reproducing in my head the movie of the possible events: the thousand

and one bifurcations that could make up the tree—split by lightning—of my biography.

But even if I do amuse myself considering that possibility, the truth is that, for the moment, I'm fine here in Argoitia's house with my twelve bromeliads. All things considered, he lets me work in peace, he's quite sweet to me, and makes an effort to understand me (although I don't think he has what it takes to do that). There are times when he even seems handsome, in a decadent kind of way; when he's gazing at the wild part of the garden while having breakfast at his wrought-iron table with peeling paint, wrapped in his cotton bathrobe, the silly smile on his face gives me a warm feeling and makes me want to kiss him. If the two of us are alone and there's no one to show off to, if he isn't in lecturer mode—speaking about the current in-vogue topic, his lips damp with wine—Argoitia lets his guard down a little and can even manage to laugh at himself. Or he recounts episodes from his childhood, when he used to climb onto the goods trains in the shunting yard of the railroad station, just by the Casino de la Selva. Stories about a city that no longer exists: a Cuernavaca with Hollywood stars and Communists. At times he makes an effort to adapt to the zeitgeist, like a bow to "us": he accompanies me to exhibitions that he invariably hates, searches the internet for new recipes to make me a dinner that doesn't include pork—I don't eat it—or grudgingly agrees to read some book I press on him: minor details that seem quite normal to me but for him are the heroic sacrifices of an enraptured lover.

Anyhow, I couldn't leave his house right now: my bromeliads love the adobe wall, the heat of the sun trap. This is the only part of the city that's still relatively humid. The wildfires are coming closer, but there's still a trickle of water in a gulley not far away and I believe the bromeliads know this, can smell it; they have an intuition that this is the only place where they are safe, misted with water like living dolls about to have their hair styled.

In the fall of 1667, in the province of Härjedalen in central Sweden, a shepherd boy called Mats had an argument with the girl who was helping him to tend the flock. The girl's name was Gertrud. It's not known what the argument was about, but I like to think that Mats tried to kiss Gertrud and she mocked her companion, who was several years younger than her and a bit dim. I imagine that Mats's childish pride was hurt and he pulled up Gertrud's skirts, or maybe insulted her or beat her legs with a stick, or perhaps he even found a dry cowpat and hurled it at her. What is clear is that the disagreement got out of hand and the twelve-year-old Gertrud hit Mats. It wasn't a very hard blow, but it was humiliating: a slap to the back of the head; a "stop-your-fooling slap" as we used to call it in my elementary school.

Mats lost his balance and ended up on his knees in the mud,

glaring at Gertrud and holding back tears of rage. Thirsting for revenge, the boy ran home and told his father what had happened. In fact, he told more than that. He claimed that after slapping and humiliating him, Gertrud had crossed the river by walking on the water, with the flock close behind, and, as if by some magic art, did it without any of them wetting their feet or sinking. Somewhere between alarmed by his son's runaway imagination and annoyed to think the girl had slapped him, Mats's father also took to his heels and ran to the parish church, where he told the whole story to the priest.

The priest summoned Gertrud to question her. Walking on water followed by thirty-nine sheep was an accusation serious enough to merit an inflexible attitude and rigorous investigation. And, indeed, the priest must have been an inflexible man—I'm not so sure about his rigor—with a great talent for persuasion: the girl not only confessed to having walked on water, but also told an extremely convoluted story about how she'd been able to do this.

According to Gertrud, when she was just eight years old, a neighbor called Märet Jonsdotter introduced her to Satan. (That's right, Satan: the old serpent, the angel of light.) And since then, she went on, Satan had taught her to fly, and Gertrud had, on several occasions, flown to the island of Blockula—described in contemporary accounts as an endless meadow (I imagine it as a barren wasteland) shrouded in mist—where she milked goats with the help of demons, participated in satanic rites, and kidnapped children.

The authorities then sought out the aforementioned Märet and took her into custody. Gertrud was also detained, awaiting trial.

In 1668, Märet Jonsdotter was brought before the court, accused of corrupting the young (as Socrates had been) and converting Gertrud and other girls—it seems that she wasn't alone in her conversion and crimes—into witches. The affair quickly became a popular topic: it was spoken of on church porches, in public squares, and the muddy markets of cities. Then more witch trials were held in other parts of Sweden. The plotline was in every instance almost the same: a boy or a group of boys accused a woman or a group of women of flying to the island of Blockula, where there was a house with a table, around which they sat to practice satanic rites under the guidance of the Devil. All cases of missing children were explained: the witches had taken them to the island. As the story was repeated, further details were added. On Blockula, it was said, the witches used to dance back-to-back and did everything in reverse: they walked backwards, had sex ass-to-ass, the way dogs sometimes do, and they also fucked Satan, whose penis was very cold. The fruits of this copulation were frogs and snakes that the women then abandoned on the island (an infinite meadow, shrouded in mist and teeming with frogs).

For eight years, the rumor grew and fear spread. Suddenly, there were more than three hundred children who had supposedly been abducted by witches, and hundreds of women were summoned to give declarations, without the hope of anyone actually listening to what they said. The show trials were followed by executions: beheaded women whose bodies were immediately incinerated. In 1675, after a mass trial held in the parish of Torsåker, sixty-five women and six men were beheaded and burned at the stake.

Even some of the boys who made the accusations ended up receiving punishment (floggings, public shamings) for having allowed themselves to be seduced by the witches. According to Joseph Glanvill's famous treatise of 1681, *Saducismus Triumphatus, or, Full and plain evidence concerning witches and apparitions. In two parts. The first treating of their possibility. The second of their real existence*, in the case of the village of Mohra, thirty-six children were condemned to be lashed on the hand once a week for a whole year. During the first weeks the lashes were administered, but as this meant the boys were unable to take part in the harvest, they began to lash them on their backs and some even had their punishment suspended.

Alarmed by the extent of the affair, the authorities convened a commission of experts to put an end to the hysteria. Sweden was at war with Denmark and the Dutch Republic (the Battle of Öland) for control of the Baltic and couldn't afford to squander its resources on the trials of hundreds of women for having sex with Satan and his cold penis. That money, they said, would be better invested in weaponry and armies. Men should be able to fight without fear that, in their hometowns and villages, their daughters were being converted into witches.

Some of the most prominent scientists and ecclesiastics of the day gathered in Stockholm in 1676 to analyze the documents of the many courts where women had been tried for witchcraft. Carl XI of Sweden had convened the most illustrious minds in his kingdom to find a solution. The Brandenburg forces were advancing from the southwest and rapid action was needed. Those men of science were required to devise a national security strategy to stop the persecution of witches in rural and more isolated areas, where the possibility of war seemed less real than satanic influences on the island of Blockula.

Among the members of the commission was the chemist and geologist Urban Hjärne, physician to the aristocracy and author of the novel *Stratonice*, published just a few years before, in which he set forth the theory that true love teaches one to chastise the impure. I guess those credentials were sufficient for his inclusion.

One group of these illustrious gentlemen proposed radical solutions, such as killing all single women over the age of thirteen in order to root out the cancer of witchcraft before, as a nation, setting out to trounce the Brandenburgers.

Another member of that council, possibly the most liberal of all, was the theologian Eric Noraeus. He led the faction of wise men who advocated for declaring all the witches innocent and so putting an end to the farce with a stroke of a pen. This was not because the cleric didn't believe in the seductive powers of the Father of Lies, but rather because the descriptions of the island of Blockula given by the accusers seemed to him highly improbable (an infinite meadow, shrouded in mist, and teeming with frogs?).

In that group of illustrious, skeptical thinkers there was also a botanist from the province of Örebro. His name was Olof Bromelius.

After deliberating for a few weeks in the sumptuous chamber of a small palace in Stockholm, the commission reached a series of preliminary conclusions. To start with, it ordered the style of the interrogations to be modified: rather than requesting the children to confirm their initial statements time after time, they were asked to repeat them. The children contradicted themselves and, eventually, retracted their accusations. From this came the modern science of interrogation, as criminologists term it, and the great Swedish witch hunt ran out of steam.

When the task of the commission of wise men was completed, the government asked priests throughout the whole country to inform their parishioners that all the witches in Sweden had been eliminated or exiled from the territory for life. Barring a few isolated cases, the persecution gradually abated over the following years and Sweden entered the modern age with a firm step, or at least that was how it seemed.

Happy to have offered his services to his country at that important moment, Olof Bromelius returned to his work as a botanist and numismatist. He made a thorough, systematic study of the flora of Gothenburg, amassed an important collection of coins, and died on February 5, 1705. The Bromeliaceae family, that is to say, bromeliads, is named in his honor.

Two nights ago, I dreamed of the witches' dance on the island of Blockula; I'd been reading about it before going to sleep. I visited the dreaded island, which, in my dream, was located in Morelos State, near Huitzilac and the Lagunas de Zempoala. There, I saw women walking in reverse, milking goats with their arms bent behind their backs, surrounded by frogs and snakes. I was woken by the mews of the cat very close to my face. I believe the smoke from the fires is putting it in an odd mood and it spends a lot of its time trying to communicate, meowing to the brown clouds or to its sleeping humans.

The German choreographer Mary Wigman would have liked the backwards dance of the witches of Blockula. Her 1914 production *Hexentanz* would have fit well in my dream.

Wigman came to dance later in life, without formal training; I sometimes think she felt the need to learn it for no other reason than to create that piece—her first composition—and so contort her body on the stage like a Blockula witch. In my opinion, except for isolated cases of virtuosos with a great many ideas, each person comes to dance in order to perform a single piece, to set a particular idea in motion. The rest of their professional careers involves delving deeper or padding out; possibly silliness.

On YouTube there's a fragment of a performance of *Hexentanz* dating from 1926. The background music was provided by cymbals and other percussion instruments (Wigman was a fan of Asian gongs, which she used for meditation), with the sound of the performer beating the boards occasionally merging with the percussion. Wigman is alone on stage, sitting on the floor throughout the whole piece. She moves toward the proscenium, but it isn't easy to see how this is done without the aid of her hands; there's something magical and inexplicable about her displacement. When Wigman performed *Hexentanz* in New York in 1931, one critic speculated that she might have an assistant hidden beneath the boards who propelled the dancer forward. It was the only possible explanation, other than demonic possession (but it would have been unacceptable to advance that hypothesis in the pages of *The New Yorker*).

At moments it seems that Wigman is suffering some kind of fit or having convulsions. Her wrists turn inward at weird angles; although the quality of the recording is poor, her features appear to contort grotesquely (though impossible, it actually happens: Wigman wore a rigid mask for the piece, so how can we see facial expressions—wood suddenly becoming a second skin?).

That piece made Mary Wigman famous and earned her a place in the history of modern dance. Despite continuing to perform until the mid-1950s, that first spark of dark genius is the most commonly remembered and frequently discussed area of her legacy.

During the First World War, Wigman took refuge in Monte Verità, a utopian—anarchist, vegetarian, and nudist—community in the Swiss canton of Ticino, where she shared her life with such members of the European cultural scene as her friend Sophie Taeuber (who was at that time working on her abstract tapestries), Hugo Ball, Pyotr Kropotkin, Rainer Maria Rilke, and the Rosicrucian Theodor Reuss, a disciple of Aleister Crowley and founder of a sect based on masonic principles known as the Ordo Templi Orientis—to which Wigman's partner at that time, the choreographer Rudolf von Laban, happened to belong. Wigman struck up a friendship with Reuss. He then introduced her to hermeticism and commissioned her to create a ritual choreography to accompany the Sonnenfest, which was to function as a kind of congress of the sect.

The residents of Monte Verità spoke Esperanto, took part in psychoanalytic sessions, and wrote frenzied manifestos. During that interval of creative freedom, while Europe was annihilating itself by means of trench warfare and gas, Wigman soaked up the spirit of the Cabaret Voltaire, but also remained loyal to her mystic interests and her curiosity about the supernatural.

In 1918, when the Great War ended, the choreographer suffered a "crisis of nerves." It's hard to say what the diagnosis would be nowadays; she'd probably be prescribed benzodiazepine and sent home. Her brother had been wounded in action and had returned an amputee. Starvation and despair were rife in Germany. Wigman separated from von Laban and, her spirit broken, had herself committed to a psychiatric clinic.

It doesn't in the least surprise me that during that crisis she began to compose her first suite of group choreographies, *Die sieben Tänze des Lebens*. I like to think that while in the sanatorium she became aware of the profound affinity between mystic rapture and the sort of possession displayed by the other female patients, which the doctors insisted on terming "hysteria." Her Faustian obsession allowed her to understand that, even in illness, there existed that inarticulable core of primitive impulses and brute sound she was attempting to channel in her art. I imagine her watching the compulsive movements of the patients, the series of ritual repetitions and the bouts of rage any interruption triggered. I picture her at a window, observing the male wing of that clinic; making rapid line drawings of the movements of war veterans hounded by hallucinations; enjoying, as she alone could, the way those interned bodies interacted, creating a secret dance nobody else saw.

If someday, after a premiere, a cultural critic from *El Diario de Morelos* asks me which choreographic style I adhere to, I'll say: The seventeenth-century Swedish witches who danced back-to-back and fucked Satan, who had a very cold penis; the women of the Weimar Republic who suffered crises of nerves, who rocked back and forth and hurled themselves at the walls under Mary Wigman's compassionate gaze. Bodies that shuffle in some mysterious way. Faces that gesticulate beneath masks. That's my choreographic style.

I've just lit a cigarette. I like smoking, but only now and again. If I smoked all the time, I wouldn't feel that sort of asphyxiation, the shortness of breath that assaults me when, every two or three days, I take a deep drag on an unfiltered cigarette.

I always smoke before eating. I enjoy feeling a little woozy, even slightly nauseated. I miss that sensation of smoking my very first cigarette: the instinctive disgust that shows your body is alive and reacting correctly. That sense of vertigo, of something being installed in your head—a fog, like the one in Blockula: mist over the infinite meadow, the croaking of frogs, women who move in reverse like fleshy crabs, without anybody being able to figure out what strange mechanism propels them.

The ashtray I use is a stone sculpture that looks like an

anthropomorphic molcajete. I've no idea where Argoitia could have gotten it. It may in fact be a sculpture made by one of his "rivals" that he decided to use as an ashtray. That's the sort of thing he does. Small, local acts of revenge. "You can't let them get away with things, Natalia," he's always saying, for no apparent reason, while we're reading or watching TV, for example.

Stuff like the ashtray is scattered all over this study. On the bookshelves, almost completely obscuring the spines of the volumes, are clay and glass pieces, photographs of Argoitia with his daughters—when they were cute identical babies, when Argoitia was still slim: twenty years ago—and photos of Argoitia with other painters (artists who died of cirrhosis, or who gave up painting to open cafés; artists who went to live in Europe and ended up working in three-star hotels in some Mediterranean town).

I find a certain pleasure in living in a house where nothing, or almost nothing, belongs to me—except the twelve bromeliads and some clothes. I feel as though I could walk out at any moment without leaving a trace, could escape to a community like the one in Ticino, Switzerland, that welcomed Mary Wigman; go to a vegetarian commune or join a cult based on masonic principles somewhere near Huitzilac and leave Argoitia to his urges, his questions, his confusion, and his cat.

The rug in the study seems to have been there for centuries. Argoitia doesn't like me smoking indoors because he says it stinks, but nothing could make the rug any worse: it smells of dust, burns, cigarettes, and time. There are cat hairs and wine stains, and other paler ones—possibly vomit—that form an abstract painting I'm capable of contemplating for hours, with the same stunned bovine stupidity as Argoitia when he's looking at his own canvases.

Behind the books on the painters of the Mexican School, at the bottom of the bookshelves, is my small hip flask of tequila. I don't keep it there to hide the fact that I drink; it's to have something of my own, a secret, a ritual I don't share. I sometimes take it out and have a swig.

I'm the only one to make any use of the books on these shelves, although I can't say I find them particularly interesting. There are three or four good works on art history that I flip through from time to time. In recent weeks, I've taken quite a liking to the one about art brut.

I'm tempted to light a second cigarette; I take one out of the pack, smell it, roll it between my fingers, and finally put it down on the table, next to the lighter and the ashtray that looks like a sculpture or a bandy-legged molcajete.

I feel like I want to cry or disappear for a while, but it isn't possible to disappear partially; in this city, people who disappear don't come back, in any shape or form.

I open my laptop and my notebook, all set to work for a while.

After recovering from her crisis of nerves, Mary Wigman fell in love with Hans Prinzhorn, a psychiatrist several years her senior. Prinzhorn, who had studied philosophy, art history, and medicine, had been an army surgeon in the Great War. Afterward, he worked in the psychiatric hospital of the University of Heidelberg, where there was a modest collection of artworks produced by the patients. Prinzhorn was excited by what he found there and decided to take charge of the collection: during his two years of curatorship, he acquired more than five thousand pieces from four hundred and fifty inmates of various European asylums. As a result, that cultural heritage came to be known as the Prinzhorn Collection.

I don't know how he and Wigman met. I like to think that, in his collector's zeal, Prinzhorn visited the sanatorium where Wigman was interned, but I have no idea if that is the case; it may just as well have been at a poetry soirée, a spinet concert, or a lecture on hypnosis. Whatever, they fell in love and lived together without being married. Prinzhorn went to work each morning at the psychiatric hospital, where he'd organized a series of art workshops for the insane: oil painting, embroidery, and clay sculpture. Every so often there would be an accident with a knife or chisel sunk into flesh, or a patient would take a slug of turps and have to be hospitalized with the painting still unfinished, but, excluding such mishaps, the workshops were an idea that bore fruit. The spirits and communicative abilities of the inmates improved, and Prinzhorn kept the creations that most interested him for his collection to add to those that colleagues sent him from such places as Amsterdam and Locarno. Occasionally, he'd allow himself a little time alone in the workshop and, after a mild dose of chloroform (in my version, he was addicted to it—as was the poet Georg Trakl—although I have no basis for that supposition), would give free rein to his artistic impulses—much more modest that Wigman's or, for that matter, his patients'.

In the same era, around 1921, the notion that art produced by the insane offered privileged access to the mechanisms of their illnesses was gaining acceptance among a variety of specialists and Prinzhorn realized that it was high time he published his findings before someone beat him to it.

Now I come to think of it, it's possible that his relationship with Wigman wasn't the master-student variety biographies claim, but one of mutual influence. The role of pedagogue is very often assigned to men in amorous relationships, particularly when the man is older, but in my own case, for example, it would be totally absurd to say that Argoitia has in any way influenced my ideas; the truth is that I'm the one who casts a discreet light onto his caveman conception of the world, when he allows it. The same might be assumed of Prinzhorn and Wigman. It's quite likely she gave him the first ideas that shaped *Artistry of the Mentally Ill: a contribution to the psychology and psychopathology of configuration* (1922), where the German psychiatrist presents and analyzes the work of ten schizophrenic artists.

Years later, in the second postwar period, Prinzhorn's collection had a profound influence on the French painter Jean Dubuffet, who also started to collect the art of the mentally ill (Argoitia's book on art brut that I often dip into has articles by Dubuffet, Prinzhorn, and Max Ernst).

As might be expected, Prinzhorn's humanistic leanings didn't sit easily with the rise of Nazism. The Nazis decided that, rather than setting them to paint pictures, it would be better to kill anyone who was different, and so they devised a eugenics program that became the model for the extermination of Jews. Prinzhorn, who died of typhoid fever in 1933, didn't survive to witness this paradigm change, although he may well have seen the writing on the wall. He'd separated from Mary Wigman some years before, but they continued to be good friends. Some of the works in his collection were included in the famous exhibition of "Degenerate Art," organized by the Nazi Party in 1937 for propaganda purposes. I like to think that among those pieces was Agnes Richter's jacket—my favorite work in the whole collection: a garment embroidered with autobiographical texts in an illegible calligraphy.

Hand-sewn jacket, embroidered with autobiographical elements and other texts. Yarn on institutional gray linen. Neck to hem 36.5 cm, Inv. 743. (In Beyond Reason: Art and Psychosis. Works from the Pronghorn Collection. *University of California Press, 1998.)*

Just as her friend Prinzhorn (and possibly even before meeting him), Mary Wigman explored the therapeutic benefits of art—dance in her case—and the idea that anyone can make art, whatever their state or condition. After all, she herself had passed through a dark period, had been subjected to the brutality of a psychiatric institution, and knew that artistic expression is capable of being, if not an escape route or salvation, at least a palliative.

I hear a car engine and automatically shut the laptop—I was searching for more information about Prinzhorn—as though I'd been looking at something illegal: but then I realize that the sound is of a car moving away, not approaching. It must be Argoitia leaving for the lunch I didn't want to accompany him to. He didn't say goodbye. Normally, he puts his head around the study door, or he might come in to give me a kiss, but things have been strained between us these last few days. First, because of the Jardín Borda. Argoitia spoke to the state's minister of culture, who spoke to the director of the Jardín Borda about a date in June to première my piece. Obviously, I didn't ask him to do that; I'm horrified by the idea of being given a space because I'm the partner of the "great painter Martín Argoitia, doyen of the arts in Morelos." Had he wangled similar things for his previous partners? Most likely. He probably thinks he's doing me a favor by getting the lakeside stage at the Borda, a horrendous place (fruit of the 1980s renovation that irreversibly ruined the last colonial-era garden in the republic) where they only ever present the state's folkloric ballet troupe.

He turned up, thoroughly pleased with himself, bursting with his news. Time to get down to work, your première is in June, he said. Get down to work. As if I required his approval, his coaching, his good intentions. I'd been getting down to work since I was sixteen, I told him. And I'd never needed anyone else to organize my productions. He was offended.

That night we went to an opening and I saw him going to the restrooms with one of the students in his workshop to do coke. His doctor—a man of the same age, but more cheerful, whom he sometimes invites to barbecues in the garden—had advised him he wasn't a youngster any longer, was overweight, and his heart wasn't what it was when he was thirty or forty. Argoitia knows this. But he also knows that it annoys me when he does coke. It's a crass drug, in my opinion, the sort bureaucrats and producers of TV commercials take; the drug of choice for people who jerk off with their socks on. Such was his small act of revenge that night: doing coke. His revenge for my not having thrown myself at his feet to thank him for having managed to get me a show on the fucking lakeside stage in the Jardín Borda. I went home early and left him to continue partying, to drown like an insecure teenager in his furious spite.

The next day he didn't wake until three in the afternoon. While I was looking through the book of art brut in the study, I heard him shuffling erratically through the house, as if he didn't know where he was. He eventually came to the study and put his head around the door. Along with the chilly air of the living room came the smell of poorly metabolized alcohol, something like acrylic paint mixed with repentance. I noticed that he was in his underwear—those white briefs with loose elastic he insists on wearing and that give him a tragic air, like a monarch who's lost his throne and his wits. I was sitting in the same armchair I'm in now, from which I can see the stains on the rug—a lunar landscape, an abstract painting—and the bromeliads on the adobe wall. (My twelve bromeliads struggling to breathe under the ashen sky of this eternal drought.) In that hoarse, nasal voice Argoitia gets when he has a hangover, he asked: Do you want me to talk to my buddy and tell him to cancel the whole thing? It was a peace offering uttered between gritted teeth, but something in me softened a little. Argoitia is proud. Naturally, he had zero desire to talk to the minister, but was willing to do so if I gave the command. In a conciliatory tone, I replied: No, what's done is done. I'll come up with something and there's still time to get the piece together, June's a couple of months off. And I guess I can spill out into the area around the stage, or do something that involves the whole garden, if they'll allow it.

Argoitia opened the door wide and came to sit by me on the floor on the disgusting rug. It gives me the giggles when he sits on the floor because he can't bend his knees and looks so uncomfortable; an albatross on dry land. As he was still in his briefs, his vulnerability was more noticeable. He rested his head on my lap, just like a dog. I unwillingly ruffled his gray hair slightly and touched his face. He hadn't shaved and the stubble had grown, but beneath that rough texture, his cheeks and double chin felt warm, as if he were running a temperature.

It's not going to be easy to find dancers for the idea I've got, I told him, although in fact I was speaking to myself. Argoitia looked at me with his lopsided smile. He understood that I'd forgiven him, just a bit. You could talk to the students at CMA, he said. I didn't reply because I didn't want to discuss my choreography with him—I didn't then and don't yet want to discuss it with anybody—but it occurred to me that the students at the Centro Morelense de las Artes were exactly the sort of dancers who'd ruin the piece I had in mind—for which I've decided to keep this sort of diary.

In the year 1900, Aleister Crowley, a scholar of religion, amateur mountaineer, and apprentice sorcerer, arrived in Mexico City from New York after a three-day train journey. His plan was to study Mexican culture, or what he imagined Mexican culture to be, and soak up a little exoticism for a few months. It was Crowley's first trip outside Europe. He had yet to found a religion or discover, in a burst of mystic enlightenment in Egypt, that he was the prophet of a new era. He had a long way to go before becoming a magus, a friend of or guide to such a diverse range of people as the Argentinian artist Xul Solar and the Portuguese poet Fernando Pessoa. Crowley was, at that time, simply an Englishman with slightly more curiosity than was the norm.

His itinerary included a secondary aim. Toward the end of

the year he planned to meet his friend and fellow mountaineer Oscar Eckenstein, with whom he was going to climb a number of Mexican peaks.

In the beginning, Crowley found Mexico deeply irritating. What little tea available was of abysmal quality. He thought the food was awful and spent several days systematically refusing to drink pulque, mezcal, or tequila (Mexicans found the concept of abstinence inconceivable). Despite all this, he rented part of a house overlooking the Alameda, in the historic center of the capital, with large rooms and exposed beams, and he soon fell in love with a Mexican woman who acted as his guide and introduced him to people. In addition, Crowley began to frequent the city's Masonic lodges.

One day, in a lodge of the "Scottish Rite," Crowley was officially initiated into Freemasonry (in a ceremony that has since been questioned). But he soon became aware that his quest required greater freedom and founded his own sect in the center of Mexico City: the Lamp of Invisible Light. To term it a sect is a slight exaggeration; in addition to Crowley, there was only one other member: a Mexican man named Jesús Medina. (Medina later moved north and, before the Revolution, took part in spiritism sessions with Francisco I. Madero.)

When Eckenstein arrived in Mexico, the first thing he did was to mock Crowley for wasting his time on frauds and Freemasons. The mountaineer respected his friend only for his climbing skills and couldn't understand his hermetic passions. Together, they ascended Iztaccíhuatl, the Volcán de Colima, the Nevado de Toluca, and, finally, Popocatépetl—where Crowley almost succumbed to altitude sickness and asked his friend to slap him repeatedly to wipe from his eyes the unspeakable visions brought on by vertigo.

I'm not certain if it was with Eckenstein or when he was traveling with his Mexican lover that Crowley made an expedition to Tepoztlán, a town that, even in those days, had a degree of fame among those interested in the paranormal, and where, eighty-seven years later, after seventeen hours in labor, my mother expelled me from her vagina.

When my father—an amateur enthusiast of the great English magus—decided family life was a middle-class imposition that didn't sit easily with his expectations of marginality, he stole my mom's savings and disappeared without a word. That was in 1989. In exchange, he left us around one hundred and fifty books. They were mainly play scripts—Beckett, Artaud, *A Doll's House*, *Spring Awakening*—plus guides to acting—two by Stanislavski and one by Grotowski—some novels from the Latin American Boom, a biography of Aleister Crowley, and various classics in those horrible two-column editions from Porrúa. I was eighteen months old when he left. By the time I reached fourteen and Mom and I had moved to Cuernavaca, the only physical souvenir I had of my father was a dozen of those books. All the others had been sold by my mother to pay off the occasional debt or were stolen by the boyfriend of the moment.

Among those remaining dozen books (I now have only the biography of Crowley, which I sometimes read aloud in that tiresome voice used by poets) there was one that I frequently perused during my teenage years, without really understanding it. It was a compilation of essays about urbanism titled *The Future City*. Some of the authors proposed fictitious cities onto which they projected their utopias (a labyrinth of small suspension bridges, a bristling esplanade of obelisks), while others chose more abstract, theoretical terrain. One of the texts was by a Dutch architect who spoke of the future city as a machine with no use. A machine whose aim would be chance, the production of accidents, anomaly. In contrast to the machines of capitalism, articulated around the notion of efficiency, the future city would have to be a poetic machine, based on notions of waste and excess, what Georges Bataille called "the accursed share." The author of that essay dedicated a section to the movement of bodies in that future city. He cited Fritz Lang's *Metropolis* and Chaplin's *Modern Times* as examples of how bodies could be moved in a machine-city programmed in function of chance and playful waste.

During my senior year of high school, I wrote an assignment for my Spanish class that was, in fact, a very thinly disguised crib of the Dutch architect's essay. Without citing my sources, I read it aloud to Mom the day before handing it in. She was moved, exclaimed how well I wrote, what original ideas I had (I thought I detected a certain tone of concern in her voice as she made the latter comment). My teacher, on the other hand, was less enthusiastic. He said my work was interesting, but it didn't fulfill the task: he'd asked us to write an "argumentative essay" with a specific structure. He gave me 75 percent, an unusually low grade for me. After class that Monday, I burned the essay. (I used to burn a lot of things in those days: it seemed the most appropriate way of getting rid of something. Now that the wildfires have besieged the city and the smoke tinges the sky a different shade each dawn, it seems to me that we should throw everything into the flames, end this farce once and for all. I guess I've always been a little melodramatic.)

I don't know what has happened to the book about the city of the future. Since I left home, Mom has dated four more men; it's not beyond the realms of possibility that one of them has taken it, or that it's gotten lost in some move, as everything does. A while back, I went to Mexico City and made inquiries about it in seven different bookstores, but none of them was willing to admit to its existence. And I haven't found anything on the internet either, so I'm starting to think that maybe it never actually existed, that I dreamed the essay about the machine-city, and dreamed the Dutch architect and his silent-movie references. But the truth is that my dreams never achieve that level of detail. In general, I dream atmospheres, colors, moving forms; at night, I free myself from plot.

Whatever the case, I'd need to find or reinvent that text about the future city for the piece I want to do in the Jardín Borda. But how?

Argoitia returned from his lunch at around nine in the evening. He was less drunk than I expected, in good humor, making jokes about the other diners. He sometimes puts a lot of effort into making me laugh and I *do* laugh, because his good humor is infectious—his witticisms, on the other hand, aren't particularly good. I asked if he wanted to watch a movie and he agreed, so long as it wasn't from Romania.

The Romanian cinema thing is a sort of private joke: when we started dating, I invited him to the Cine Morelos to see a Romanian movie I was interested in. He accepted the invitation; at the beginning of a relationship, you try to seem flexible. It wasn't a good movie, but not that bad either. There were a lot of explicit sex scenes between two men and Argoitia began to get edgy, wriggling in his seat like a child in a waiting room. As we were just beginning to get to know each other, I asked if he wanted to leave. Nowadays, I'd never suggest leaving a theater because he didn't like the movie, but there we are. We went to a nearby mezcal bar and later to his house. It was the first time I spent the night with him here in this house, which is partially my house now, or at least the home of my twelve bromeliads.

But all that about watching or not watching Romanian cinema is wearing thin. One more stain with a backstory, like the multitude of others on the rug in the study. A relationship can at times take the form of a modern city constructed on the vestiges of extinct civilizations: there are still traces, names, stones belonging to that idyllic past, but your focus is mainly on the unbearable traffic of the present, on the brownish clouds from nearby fires.

I told Argoitia to put on anything he wanted, because I knew he'd drop off in no time at all—he didn't sleep last night—and then I could watch something else.

When I'm working on a project, everything seems to fall into line: coincidental connections begin to appear in my memories, in what I'm reading, my conversations, and the movies I watch, allusions that are added to the system of false starts and intuitions I'm constructing in this notebook. It's so exciting to read the first four lines of a book and immediately know it's exactly the book you need to read at that precise moment. The world ceases to be the hostile place it almost always is, filled with bad, ignorant people, and becomes an endless meadow, like the island of Blockula, where I can move around at will, surrounded by crab-women. Paths open up before me like ripe mangos trickling the sweet syrup of Truth, and I can eat and get my face and hands dirty, like a rosy-cheeked child having the time of her life.

Argoitia fell asleep and I closed the ridiculous blockbuster he'd chosen and put on a German, or maybe Austrian movie. Here's the plot: a woman of around forty is traveling by intercity train to a business meeting. She's sitting by the window with the tray table down, underlining a document.

At some point, the train goes through a tunnel and the woman looks up from her papers as the interior lights haven't been switched on; it's dark and she can't go on reading. On the window, the reflection of the inside of the car is superimposed on the cement walls of the tunnel on the other side of the glass. The woman sees her own reflection, but the movement of the train and the artificial lighting distort the image and she sees something else in the window that she can't quite locate inside or outside: a person falling like a newly felled tree. Startled, the woman turns around but can't see anything inside the car and so attributes the event to some sort of optical illusion. The train leaves the tunnel and the woman starts working again, but it's clear that the image of the falling body is still on her mind, that she can't quite shrug it off, so she puts away her papers and walks to the dining car. She takes a seat opposite a man who immediately asks if she's going to Vienna. The woman gives an evasive answer, she obviously has no desire to get into conversation with a stranger. But the man returns to the attack with fresh questions. She stands rather brusquely, excuses herself, and returns to her seat, where the swaying of the train rocks her to sleep. When she wakes, the train is quiet and she looks out the window to see what station they are in, but finds they have stopped in the middle of the countryside. A number of rumors circulate among the passengers in her car about what has happened; apparently, they have been there for ten minutes. Some are saying that there's been an attack, others that it's a problem on the track. Finally, one rumor gains prominence: there's been some kind of accident. The woman goes to the bathroom to splash water on her face because she's had a disturbing dream that still seems to be gummed to her eyelids. On her way, she finds one of the train doors open and, almost automatically, decides to go outside. She walks toward the front of the train and discovers that there is a body lying by the tracks. She looks on from a prudent distance and realizes that it's the man who was asking her questions in the dining car.

I don't remember the rest of the movie in much detail.

Coincidences are like oysters opening simultaneously, a choir of bivalves intoning the song of meaning. The first coincidence opens, offers up its pearl; the others don't want to be left behind.

This morning Argoitia fell in the shower and broke his arm. He squealed like a pig subjected to the cruel practices of the meat industry and I remembered that I'd only ever seen him cry once, and that was before I moved in with him. We'd had sex three times that day—a miracle at his age—and he'd told me he'd never felt so alive. I knew that was an exaggeration or a lie, something he'd said many times before, but I still liked the fact that he said it, because things can be false and true at the same time, and, in his tears, I saw that it was true too.

Still wailing from the fall, with his arm hanging at an impossible angle, Argoitia asked me to drive him to the hospital, but I haven't driven for years and was too frightened to try, so I called a cab. While we were waiting for it to arrive, Argoitia downed half a bottle of tequila in a couple of gulps, even though I told him it wasn't a good idea to have alcohol in his bloodstream in case he needed medication.

On the whole, I react badly to other people's crises. The energy needed to pay so much attention to their dramas is totally draining and puts me in a foul mood. At the hospital, I was distant and eventually told Argoitia that I'd go home while they were taking the X-rays. He gave me a reproachful look but, as was his custom, didn't say anything (he'd make me pay for it in his own way later). When I got back to the house, what I wanted to do was water the bromeliads and sit a while with them, but the wind had changed direction and the smoke from the fires felt more than usually heavy in my lungs, so I made do with looking at them from the study window.

I suspect that Olof Bromelius died without ever seeing the plants named after him. His specialty was the flora of Gothenburg, while bromeliads are to be found on the American continent. It was his compatriot Carl Linnaeus, born two years after Olof's death, who paid tribute to him when outlining the features of bromeliads in his *Species Plantarum*. The first bromeliad Linnaeus describes is the pineapple, which, he says, is native to Nueva España and Suriname.

For his part, Olof amassed some of the most impressive collections of his day: an incomparable assemblage of coins and another of botanical specimens. On his death, his son Magnus Bromelius inherited the collections and continued to enlarge them. Father and son shared a fascination for coins but, in contrast to Olof, Magnus preferred rocks to plants. His collection of minerals was greatly admired throughout Sweden and, possibly to keep his father's memory alive without neglecting his own interests, Magnus included plant fossils in his research. Bromellite, an oxide mineral discovered in Sweden in 1925, owes its name to him.

I'd like to have bromellites too. Bromeliads and bromellites: plants and oxides whose forms I can admire while the fire moves closer.

I've been thinking a lot about the book on the future city I inherited from my father when he left. If I had to invent a fictional city, an absurd machine-city where the space was organized in function of chance and surplus, the basic movement of bodies in that city would be falling, stumbling, the vertical descent traced out by the bromeliad I found in the forest.

"He who stumbles but doesn't fall, gains ground," is one of the adages my mom heard from my grandmother and loves repeating (without always understanding their possible meanings). But the person who stumbles and falls gains nothing: the impetus is wasted.

Falling, stumbling, vanishing: bodies that return to earth when least expected. Did the woman on the train in the

Austrian movie get a glimpse of the future when she saw the reflection of someone falling onto the track? And had Argoitia in some way foreseen his fall—his slide down in the shower—before breaking his arm?

In Strasbourg, in the summer of 1518, Frau Troffea—then nineteen or twenty years old—suddenly began to dance in the middle of the street, without music or accompaniment, rhyme or reason. Some sources say that she kept it up for days, until she finally succumbed to exhaustion; however, she soon recovered and, despite the sores on her feet, began to dance again.

Initially, people looked at her in surprise and then went about their business. They had seen worse. A second woman witnessed Frau Troffea's movements and felt the urge to join her, so she didn't have to dance alone, or perhaps to stop the townsfolk censuring that unheard-of behavior: it would be less strange if two were dancing together.

According to the alchemist Paracelsus, who visited Stras

bourg in 1526 to investigate the event, Frau Troffea had started dancing following an argument with her husband.

Paracelsus is to the dancing plague of 1518 what Linnaeus is to the Swedish witch hunts of the next century: the illustrious wise man who turns up years later to put things in order and assign responsibility, and—invariably—finds that it's all the fault of the women (for being silly and superstitious, to piss off their husbands). But some authors—John Waller in *The Dancing Plague*, for instance—say that Frau Troffea didn't dance to piss off her husband, but because she'd experienced famine, owed money, and was suffering afflictions. The Church had gradually taken possession of all the arable land around Strasbourg, and profiteering priests hoarded food during droughts to inflate prices. Before Frau Troffea took to dancing, many people were forced to wander homeless through the countryside of Europe after their homes had been seized. Maybe that was why Frau Troffea danced: because she owed money to a priest, had eaten very little, and two of her children had been carried off by dysentery; because it hadn't rained for months—like now—and the cows had stopped giving milk and the hens laying eggs. Whatever the case, when Frau Troffea started to dance something was wrong in her life, and in the life of the woman who decided to accompany her, in the lives of the majority of the inhabitants of Strasbourg in those years of poor harvests.

Perhaps the second woman who began to dance had had an argument with her husband too, as Paracelsus wrote; she may also have had little food or lost a child, she may have eaten rye bread past its best, bread with the mold of a certain fungus with a molecular structure similar to LSD. It's impossible to say. Paracelsus came to his own conclusions, but, if the alchemist will forgive me, they sound kind of stupid.

Frau Troffea and the second woman danced together for a while, but they were very soon joined by others: young women ravaged by hunger and depraved by violence, descendants of the last victims of the Bubonic plague. They danced on, and soon men began to accompany them, just a few, almost all boys who had worked with those same women and had cried with them when their possessions were lost to usury ("Corpses are set to banquet at behest of usura," writes Ezra Pound in his most famous Canto, which brings to mind those medieval prints depicting the Dance of Death).

In less than a week, fifty people were dancing in the streets of Strasbourg. The doctors decided that it would be best to wait for them to tire, and even encouraged them to go on dancing to hurry on that moment. They sent for musicians to follow the procession of frenetic dancers; the musicians tired but the dancers continued. They danced for days without stopping to eat a mouthful or drink water. People began to ask how they managed it. Were they possessed by the Devil? Hexed by some macabre spell? The bodies of the dancers started to show signs of weariness, and around the middle of the second week, the first deaths occurred. Frau Troffea had taken to her bed several days before, unable to remember anything of the events, but the movement she'd initiated had a life of its own, a death of its own. The first woman who had decided to accompany her suffered a fatal heart attack; and a blacksmith's son, a boy of thirteen who was to be married the following week, was also found dead on the outskirts of the city—his blond hair matted with mud. And others died, but their deaths did nothing to calm the epidemic. For every fallen dancer, three more joined the throng. Some danced slightly apart, their backs turned to the others, as though sunk in their own concerns. Others cried and laughed—at the same time—as they danced, leering at their companions. Certain sources indicate that many men took advantage of the strange epidemic to display their genitals and make obscene movements near the women, pretending to be infected by the disease. But then they really did catch it and, with their dicks hanging out, began to contort themselves without any sexual intention. A few fell dead after a couple of days, overcome by thirst and the July heat.

The 1518 choreomania or dance epidemic in Strasbourg wasn't the first such episode. There are reports of similar cases throughout the Late Middle Ages. In 1374, in Aix-la-Chapelle, the same thing happened: a group of people began to dance spontaneously, holding hands in circles. The dancers appeared oblivious to everything around them; it was as if they had lost control of their limbs. They danced on until, a few days later, they dropped from exhaustion. Witnesses of that strange spectacle ran to help the victims, who were moaning in agony on the ground, and bound cloths tightly around their waists to relieve the pain. Once they had recovered, the dancers declared that they had seen visions. Some said they felt they had been carried in a strong current of blood, as if they were swimming in a crimson river that obliged them to leap upward. Others saw the skies open and the Savior and the Virgin Mary sitting on thrones above them—spectators in a royal box, contemplating the unhappy theater of human passions, the broken hips of their sad dancing puppets. In the same year, fresh outbreaks were reported in Liege, Utrecht, Bruges, and Antwerp. In some places, the afflicted were locked in taverns or stables. In other, more inventive places, they decided that the best treatment was to kick and punch them in the hope of expelling the demons from their bodies. A number of people died from the cure rather than the illness itself.

There are incidental reports of symptoms that were exhibited only in certain locations. In Liege, the dancers were irritated by the sight of the color red, which aroused them even further. In another small Flemish town, it was said that the victims of the paroxysm couldn't bear the presence of people who were crying. In Utrecht, the priests carried out exorcisms, with little success, and they then banned the use of pointed shoes, convinced they had something to do with the whole business.

The strange fever spread farther afield, from one city to another: Cologne, Maastricht, Leuven. Vagabonds learned to imitate the contortions of those affected and used this skill to travel through Europe in search of adventures. They would arrive in a town, dance for a few hours, steal a chicken, and continue on their way.

But even that episode of the strange fever was not the first example of choreomania. The same had happened in 1278, on a bridge near Utrecht, where the spontaneous dancers leaped about and skipped until the foundations of the bridge collapsed; they were all drowned. And before that, in 1237, in Erfurt, a group of children began to dance and leap along the road without anyone being able to stop them. And even earlier, in 1027, in the church in Kolbig, a number of people interrupted a mass with their convulsions. I read all this in a book by Justus Friedrich Carl Hecker, *The Dancing Mania of the Middle Ages* (first published in Berlin in 1832); I found a PDF on the internet after surfing for a couple of hours and read it sitting on the disgusting rug in the study, taking sips of tequila from my flask.

At some point while I was reading, I dozed off—the laptop on the coffee table, my head resting on the side of the armchair, the cat watching me from a corner of the bookshelves, which it loves to climb. It can't have been more than a fifteen-minute nap. The ringtone of my phone startled me awake and I answered confusedly, not really understanding who was calling as I hadn't checked the name glowing on the screen. It was Conejo. As usual, he launched into a monologue about his latest discoveries without even saying hello. He'd found a punk band from Jiutepec with a name he thought was awesome: Shitty Toilet Paper. And, he claimed, he'd thought of ringing me because he knew just how much I'd appreciate that information. And without even a segue, he went on to read out the full list of songs on the band's only album, a garage CD Conejo had just bought (he has a weird fetish about that dreadful, obsolete technology that no one else uses): "Nose Cotton," "Zombie Wasps," "Yellow Hotel," "Pulling Punches" . . . I told him that his call had woken me, that I hadn't the least idea what he was talking about, what was going on. Conejo emitted that engaging but slightly silly laugh he's had forever and asked if I was tired of married life yet. I'm not married, you cretin, I answered with a smile. But I *am* tired; I can't sleep.

Conejo is the nearest thing to a childhood friend I still have. We met in high school, at the Arcadia, and he's the only person who understands and shares my love/hate relationship with Cuernavaca.

I told him that Argoitia had broken his arm, and also that he'd gotten me a show in the Jardín Borda, on the lakeside stage. Another loud laugh: And what are you going to do, *Swan Lake*? Maybe I should, I replied. A gore version where all the ballerinas are menstruating and their pink tutus gradually acquire bloodstains during the performance. Conejo loved the idea and amused himself talking about that hypothetical piece for a few minutes. He said that as a finale I could pull a lever that would tip a huge tub of red paint over the audience. Then, in the same abrupt way he'd started the call, he said he had to go and hung up without giving me time to say another word. I guess he was feeling alone and needed company. He lives with his blind father in the house where he grew up and rarely goes out. As far as I know, the only people he speaks to are me and his dealer, who brings him Morelense punk CDs and bags of marijuana.

Conejo gave me one of my favorite bromeliads, the *Neoregelia*. It's among the ones growing in a planter and has a really large water tank. The leaves are green and white, but just before it flowers the center of the plant, around the tank, turns dark red, which is why I call it my menstruating plant. The red coloration acts as an interspecies lure: insects can't resist the sight of that exuberant, lubricious color and dip their heads into the reddish center of the plant to pollinate it.

It suddenly occurs to me that there's a certain resemblance to the medieval choreomanias in the way mosquitos succumb to the *Neoregelia*: an attraction to the red that also repels, a fall to the bottom of the dark liquid from where there is no return.

With his arm immobilized, Argoitia is unbearable. He wanted an old-fashioned plaster cast (he has these fixations), but in the hospital they told him they were no longer in use and fitted one of those light synthetic splints. As he broke his right arm, he's started a painting series of hideous canvases with his left, which he can't even use to wipe his ass. The result leaves a lot to be desired, but I long ago learned not to tell him what I think of his art; better to avoid hard feelings. He's convinced that these canvases will later form a *period*; he can almost imagine a collector obsessed with the idea of tracking down the last painting from his *left-hand period*. Poor man. Yet maybe his fantasy isn't completely crazy: the mechanisms through which a person enters the canon in this country are so unfathomable there's no point in trying to understand them.

If only he'd be as serious about the challenge of doing everything else with his left hand instead of asking for my help in carrying out the most basic tasks: making coffee in the mornings, dressing, taking a shower with a plastic bag around his arm. Luckily, the day after tomorrow he's going to the opening of a retrospective of his work, organized by a gallery in San Miguel de Allende. He invited me along, but I told him I'd sooner be tried for witchcraft in seventeenth-century Sweden. He didn't appreciate my sarcasm.

I took advantage of those solitary days to make a few sketches for the choreography of the performance in the Jardín Borda. I now have a provisional title: *The Great Noise*, which is the name given to the period of collective hysteria and witch hunts in Swedish history. It will be my personal tribute to the satanic rites on Blockula, to Mary Wigman, and to Frau Troffea, who sparked off the 1518 dance epidemic in Strasbourg.

Argoitia will most likely get mad at me about the piece. He's never been to any of my performances and I guess he believes I'm a more or less conventional choreographer, like all the other prissy women that have done the CMA's dance diploma. He might end up having problems with the minister of culture, but then I never asked him to get the lakeside stage for me.

The island of Blockula does in fact exist and is located in the Baltic Sea. Its real name is Blå Jungfrun, the Blue Maiden. Legend has it that witches would assemble there every Maundy Thursday. When Linnaeus visited the place in 1741, he used the occasion and his Enlightenment reasoning to ridicule the superstitions surrounding the island. But he also noted that it was a horrendous place, one of the harshest and bleakest landscapes on earth, and so it was unsurprising that those morbid tales had occurred to his compatriots.

When it comes to pioneers of scientific knowledge in Sweden's Early Modern Period, I'm more of a fan of Olof Bromelius than the insufferable Linnaeus.

In *Saducismus Triumphatus*, Glanvill brings together a number of testimonies about Blockula. According to one of them, Satan gave the witches two animals; one the size of a young cat that they call the Carrier, and the second a "bird as big as a Raiven, but white." The witches would send these creatures out to forage for provisions: butter, cheese, milk, and bacon. Whatever the albino crow found, they could keep for themselves, but all the food brought by the cat had to be given to the Devil, who stored it in Blockula to be distributed among his acolytes as he saw fit.

Sometimes, when I go to the supermarket, I imagine an enormous white bird and a young cat picking out bacon in the meat section.

Conejo came over for a few beers this evening, taking advantage of Argoitia's departure for San Miguel de Allende yesterday. I'm always trying to make plans that include them both, but they are having none of it: they can't stand each other and are incapable of sharing a space without indulging in veiled attacks.

Conejo despises the figure Argoitia cuts: we've been seeing his name in the culture section of the city's newspaper, in gallery programs, and among the teaching staff of cultural workshops since we were in our teens. For Conejo, Argoitia represents that local small-time mafia we used to make fun of between classes at the Arcadia, and that was why a number of our friends went to study and find jobs in Mexico City. For Argoitia, Conejo represents—even more than I do—an ungrateful generation that fails to recognize his importance, that doesn't roll out the red carpet for his prizes or applaud his honorary mentions in the painting biennials he's so laboriously managed to achieve in the course of his life. Conejo, for Argoitia, is the face of a lazy, patricidal generation that criticizes without producing anything itself, that doesn't get its hands dirty but uses social media platforms to launch its barbs of so-called marginal purity. That's how he explains it, but in more abusive language, although he does then repent because he'd prefer not to care, to enjoy the flattery that goes with power without worrying about what younger people think. But the truth is, he can't.

Personally speaking, the rivalry between them doesn't bother me and I don't take sides. While I'm more inclined to understand the world from Conejo's viewpoint, that perspective also seems to me a little stupid and I feel there's no point in identifying too closely with the zeitgeist. I'm certain that in fifteen years, or even sooner, the younger generation will be looking down on me and mocking my artistic stance, and instead will believe that the tacky romanticism and technical refinement of Argoitia's generation have been unjustly undervalued. Time is cyclical, and its only aim is to fuck us all up.

Conejo was armed with three large bottles of beer: It's bad luck to drink in even numbers, he said. He's full of odd tics and beliefs like that. If he'd lived in seventeenth-century Sweden, he'd have sworn that the witches took him to Blockula and made him dance backwards. If he'd lived in Strasbourg in 1518, Conejo would have been the sort of priest who carried out exorcisms on possessed dancers, to Paracelsus's absolute despair.

He told me that his father was learning to read Braille.

Conejo orders things online for him—simple books, for children and young adults—and Señor Bertini reads them alone in his study. Sometimes Conejo hears him laughing aloud, but when he comes out to make Turkish coffee, his expression is somber. I find it moving to imagine that pigheaded old man rediscovering his own laughter while reading "Little Red Riding Hood" with his fingers.

Conejo also informed me that Erre—the first boy I dated and a fellow student at the Arcadia—returned to Cuernavaca a while back. He made a real fanfare of it, calculating that the news would matter to me more than it did. I haven't seen Erre for three years and haven't spent more than half an hour talking to him in the last decade. True, there was a time when his love and his betrayal formed a kind of schism for me, a rite of passage for entering the world of heterosexual relationships, with their habitual dose of frustration and violence, but so many things have happened since then that, with the benefit of hindsight, I can only say it was an adolescent affair, with all the drama and intensity that implies.

I don't bear Erre any grudges, but neither do I have tender feelings for him, above all because I perceive a discontinuity in my own life that means I find it very hard to identify with the person I was ten or fifteen years ago. (At times I even find it hard to identify with the person I was eight months ago, two weeks, ten minutes ago: my identity is a rodeo bull that bucks and jumps around the ring, throwing off anyone who tries to mount it.)

Conejo returned to the topic of my performance in the Jardín Borda. Sounding more serious than he had on the phone, he asked if I was thinking of doing something weird, spilling out of the assigned space to toy with the audience. He knows me, and is highly intuitive, although it isn't a talent he generally makes much use of. I said I was thinking of a new-age dance, something related to trances, possession, episodes of collective hysteria, to rumor and the way it twists things out of shape. He attempted to get a few concrete details from me—Someone pisses on the stage? he asked—but I changed the subject and passed him a beer bottle to open with his teeth (as he always proudly does, even when he has a bottle opener in his hand).

Erre had been a good-looking teenager, very good-looking, with the sort of beauty that, glimpsed casually, out of the corner of your eye, could seem like ugliness. He developed a severe case of acne at an early age, but it soon disappeared and left him with a pockmarked complexion that made him look older than he was and a little bit evil, somehow weathered. He had a cubist profile, long hair, and the shifty gaze of a fugitive. When he was sixteen, he decided he was going to be a movie director and carried a photographic camera around with him everywhere, although I think that was just for show: I never saw him take a single shot. His interventions in class tended to be slightly aloof, as though his aim was to demonstrate the teacher's ignorance rather than his own progress or the breadth of his ideas. But even so, he'd sometimes astonish the rest of us. There was a mocking curl to his lips when he was debating something; he'd convert words into spangles that, in the artificial lighting of the classrooms, seemed like precious minerals.

That was my initial impression. When I began talking to him, however, I had the feeling that his intelligence was too literal and accumulative, that there was no mystery about him. I also thought that if his intelligence didn't develop some form of sensibility, it was in danger of withering. Lots of men are like that; they seem brilliantly intelligent for a moment, and then you realize they are databases, learned formulas and cast-iron convictions that, like anything ferric, end up rusting on contact with life. Intelligence without self-doubt is about as much use as a chocolate coffee pot. I had a suspicion of all that back then, but the first rush of teenage hormones clouded my judgment.

We started dating in the second year of high school and soon decided to use the Easter vacation to go away somewhere together. Erre told his parents he was traveling to Acapulco with a friend and his family; I told my mom the truth (I was never much good at coming up with stories): I was going to Oaxaca with my boyfriend. At the downtown bus terminus, it suddenly occurred to us that we might not be allowed to travel without an adult, that we'd be asked for proof of age before boarding the bus. Erre was in much more of a flap than me, to the point of wanting to call off the trip. A little surprised by his lack of courage, I told him to do whatever he wanted, but I was going to Oaxaca. At the very last minute, he nervously boarded the bus with me, cursing under his breath.

My adolescence was very much like my childhood, but with the addition of libido: I enjoyed riling the boys, but then I'd repent because what I really wanted was to kiss them. On the bus to Oaxaca, I spent half an hour teasing Erre about his fear of lying to his parents and of coming away with me.

I thought banter was our way of getting along, but I didn't realize I was taking it too far: Erre burst into tears of pure rage. He yelled that I was an idiot, an accusation I've never forgiven. I was dumbstruck. These days, I'd slap the face of anyone who insulted me and cold-shoulder them from then on, but at that time, having grown up with an absent father, I wasn't used to those angry put-downs from men. I tried to snuggle up to him, stroke his hair, kiss him on the lips, but Erre's pride was hurt and he pushed me away, wiping his tears on the frayed sleeve of his denim jacket. After a period of silence, he closed his eyes and I thought he was asleep. I watched him as he dozed, frightened I'd messed up my first relationship before it had really begun. Luckily, Erre woke up in a calmer mood. He kissed my neck and acted like nothing had happened.

The trip to Oaxaca was an initiation. We lost our respective virginities in the metal bed of a very uncomfortable cheap hotel and Erre got so drunk on mezcal that he passed out on a bench (a kindly local brought him a mug of instant coffee and made him drink it). The experience brought us closer and, as one does, we swore undying love. We also swore loyalty to our chosen careers and made a pact that if either of us ended up working in an office instead of becoming an artist, the other would never talk to him (or her) again.

When we got back to Cuernavaca, it turned out that his parents had discovered his lie (that he wasn't in Acapulco under the care of two responsible adults), with the result that I was branded a bad influence (which was true) and he was made to wash the family car once a week for four months. Before he'd completed his punishment, we'd split up. What happened was that Erre had gotten drunk and made out for half an hour with a girl from the year below us at a party I couldn't attend because I'd just had my tonsils removed. As was to be expected, someone from the Arcadia told me and I broke things off over the phone—my voice doubly insecure due to the lemon ice cream that had frozen my tongue and the fact that it was the first time anything like that had happened to me.

We continued in the same class for a year until graduation. Erre moved to Mexico City and I stayed in Cuernavaca to study dance and collect bromeliads. As far as I know, Erre's ambitions never bore fruit. His intelligence dried up, just as I'd predicted, and he gradually narrowed his horizons. He flunked the university entrance exam for film studies three times; then he had to start paying rent and found a job in a production company whose greatest success was a commercial for hemorrhoid cream. We hadn't been in touch for ages by then, so there was no need to worry about our pact.

When Conejo left at about ten, I was feeling wide awake, as almost always happens when I drink beer. I tried hugging the cat in bed but it's a slightly crotchety feline and scratched my arm. After tossing and turning in the tangle of blankets for a couple of hours, checking my phone every five minutes, I got up, put on a pair of pants, and went to the study. I lit a cigarette but had to stub it out after a couple of puffs because my chest hurt. I think the smoke from the fires is as much as my lungs can take.

After that, I reread my notes for the choreography and some of the pages I'd printed out about medieval dance plagues. (Printing out articles to read later is an outdated absurdity I cling to, just like Conejo and his CDs.) With that febrile lucidity of sleeplessness, I jotted down a few instructions for the prospective dancers and then went to the kitchen.

I made coffee at around 5 a.m. and, wrapped in Argoitia's bathrobe—it smelled of his sweat and shaving cream—went out onto the terrace to watch the sun come up. But it didn't. Night dragged on for what felt like an eternity and I even thought it had been hasty to draw the logical conclusion that day would break just because it always had before. I heard a noise coming from the withered trees in the least pretty area of the garden, maybe a cacomixtle, and decided to go back to bed and write this.

At night, Argoitia's house sometimes frightens me a little. The wind lashes the branches of a tree against the window, making an ominous sound. And what's more, the smoke from nearby wildfires clusters densely around the streetlight, letting in a purplish glow, like in a Mexican horror film from the seventies.

In addition to the many adages my grandmother taught my mother, she also told her a number of scary stories, which Mom in turn has told me. My absolute favorite is the one about the witches who had lived near her hometown (a municipality in Mexico State that eventually merged with Toluca). In my grandmother's story, the witches had false legs that could be "unscrewed," as my mother said my grandmother put it. On St. John's Eve they would remove—"untwist"—their legs and dance in the hills, emitting flames from the waist down, as if they had become some kind of human firecracker. Those flames were, according to my mother—who had it from her mother—will-o'-the-wisps.

My grandmother was sent to a boarding school in Toluca when she was twelve. She was very short for her age and the other children made fun of her, cut her hair when she was asleep, and played all kinds of dirty tricks on her. My mother told me that Grandma started telling those tales about the witches at night, and she was such a good storyteller that the other girls would be unable to sleep, tormented by the images. The next day, her abusers would be found wandering like lost souls along the school corridors, dark shadows under their eyes, and as the mere sight of my grandmother reminded them of her stories, they avoided her at all costs. So, thanks to her ability to tell horror stories, my grandmother made it through school.

It isn't easy to visualize the witches who took off their legs and danced while emitting flames from their waists, but I've been thinking over that legend I like so much. If my grandmother were alive, I'd ask for more details. Sadly, I only have that strange fragment of the story passed down through the generations. Mom didn't inherit my grandmother's gift for storytelling: she tells it all with the same over-the-top fervor that makes it vague, or she dwells on the weak points of the story and skips the important bits.

Maybe I should include the fiery witches of Toluca in the performance. Maybe Grandma should be there too.

I was sixteen when I first saw Argoitia. At that time, he was a handsome, tormented forty-something. My dance class in the basement of the CMA had just finished and I was walking along the upper corridors of the center—a hospital in a previous incarnation—peeking into the rooms as I passed. I saw him through the half-open door of one of the workshops. Argoitia was standing over a huge white canvas that had been spread on the floor. At his feet, five students were painting different areas of the cloth and the scene made me think of a feudal lord overseeing the sowing of crops on his land in the early spring. Argoitia spotted me in the doorway and stared, almost reprovingly. I ran off.

He claims not to recall that first meeting, or the second, a few weeks later, in the Cine Morelos. The main salon was in a former theater, the sort where the stalls are huge, and it was so poorly maintained that a family of bats had taken up residence in an area of the ceiling. At times, halfway through the movie, you'd see the flapping wings of an errant bat cross the screen, and, inevitably, a woman would scream. But for the regular clientele of the Cine Morelos, those animals were part of the attraction.

That day, Erre and I had gone to see an entry in the International Film Festival and Argoitia was in the row ahead of us with the girl he was dating just then. I don't remember what the movie was. Erre was focused on the screen. My attention was elsewhere; I'd recognized Argoitia and was spying on him; on him and his companion. In the bluish dark of the salon, I was able to make out that they were touching each other, or rather Argoitia had his hand under the woman's skirt, while she sat there, apparently unperturbed. In those days, my sex life was limited to those necking sessions with Erre—slightly clumsy, almost always at my place, with my mother watching a movie in the next room. Seeing Argoitia secretly feeling up a woman in public was a disturbingly contradictory experience. I can't say that I was exactly aroused, but I later dreamed—repeatedly, and in a nightmarish kind of way—that I was the one Argoitia was feeling up in that gloomy theater, with a thousand bats flying around us.

After that, I didn't see him again for a few years. Shortly after the episode in the movie theater came the trip to Oaxaca and then I split up with Erre. The following year, I graduated from high school and began the dance diploma in the same building as I'd studied classical and contemporary ballet: the Centro Morelense de las Artes. But by then, Argoitia had stopped teaching there (due to some political in-fighting, as I later learned): he'd holed up in his house, this house, to paint a series of large-format oils that fleetingly gave fresh life to his career—they were exhibited in Monterrey and in a collective show at the Museo de la Estampa in Mexico City.

During those years, my love life entered a phase that I still sometimes miss: I had occasional lovers (a pseudo musician, a charlatan who used to say he was trying to find himself, a small-time criminal) and earned a reputation for being weird and wicked in the spineless circles of local culture, where anyone who cries in public is branded crazy.

Dawn finally broke. I made more coffee and returned to the study. When I haven't slept all night, I often feel vulnerable, but also receptive, as though I were tuning in more clearly to that radio frequency of pink noise that some people like to call inspiration. But this time I was quite simply feeling tired. I spent two hours on Wikipedia while outside it rained ash.

I read about bromeliads. The largest species, *Puya raimondii*, can reach over fifty feet in height; from a distance, it could be mistaken for some species of agave. It is found only in the Andes, at about ten thousand feet above sea level. In contrast to the *Tillandsia* that I recently found in the forest, the puya—also known as the *Titanka raimondii* (a name I'd give my daughter if I had one)—grows in earth. It is a monocarpic plant: the male of the species dies after a single reproductive event. A puya can live more than a hundred years, which suggests that some pass a whole century waiting to have sex; then they blossom, scatter their seeds, and die.

I've decided on a number of elements of the choreography. The most important is that, despite Argoitia's intervention, it won't be staged in the Jardín Borda, but throughout the whole city. Now I have to start auditioning dancers. I'm going to place classified advertisements in the *Informador de Morelos*: "People of all ages wanted for a dance performance. Paid work. Dancing skills unnecessary," with my phone number below. That should attract a few candidates. I haven't posted the announcement on my social media groups because I think it will work better among readers of a print newspaper: I'm curious to see what types of specimen reply to an advertisement like that.

A neighbor here has a jackass that sometimes makes very strange noises; all the other jackasses I've heard speak differently.

•

Sonia, the only friend I made while studying at the CMA, called me today. She gave up dancing some time ago and, as far as I know, she's now a full-time parent, but we've kept in touch and she's the only person I can bear to have long phone conversations with. I get impatient with anyone else, including Conejo, after a few minutes and quickly end the call, but Sonia is different. I find the tone of her voice calming, plus she has a sense of humor—often directed at herself—that fits very well with mine. I also believe that when we talk, she unburdens herself and tells me all the things she keeps from her family. Today, for instance, she confessed that when she bathes her youngest daughter—a two-year-old—she likes putting a little of the soap lather in her mouth just to see the disgusted faces she pulls. Only a little lather, she said, it doesn't harm her. Details like that make Sonia one of my favorite people.

I don't know how the hell it happened, but Sonia had heard that I was preparing a performance for the Jardín Borda. She wouldn't say who told her. I guess the rumor finally spread among my former classmates. Sonia told me that there's a certain amount of speculation about what I'm going to do next: it seems I have a reputation for eccentricity among the fifteen people who attend contemporary dance performances in Morelos State. I have the sense that my friend wanted me to tell her what I was planning so she could experience a vicarious form of excitement (she once aspired to being a choreographer too). Instead of fobbing her off, I decided to offer an invitation: Why not join the company and see for yourself? I promised it wouldn't take up too much of her time: instead of actual rehearsals, I'd be doing something that could loosely be described as workshops over three weekends before casting the roles; what I most wanted was to talk to the dancers, read them some articles, and carry out guided improvisations, but in her case I could fit in with her schedule and see her separately if necessary. Sonia initially said she didn't think she'd be able to do it, said she hadn't danced in years and after having given birth twice her body wasn't in the same condition as when we were students. I explained that my choreographies were for bodies with history, not pixies and sprites. Sonia accepted the invitation and thanked me multiple times, which made me feel magnanimous.

I have moments of self-doubt. Why make so much effort for no purpose? Maybe I should focus on beautiful, conventionally graceful pieces; set aside these idiotic notes and assume the flat immediacy of prettiness. I don't have a particularly interesting life. The only good reason I have for being a choreographer is a tendency to think in terms of movement, the body, and space. My insights are often impossible to communicate: private epiphanies in the bromeliad garden, sighs breathed alone after taking a swig from my flask. Apart from those isolated, unrepeatable instants, you could say I'm a phony. My sadness—my impatience—is the sadness of the scientist who discovers how to produce electricity but still can't store it or change the voltage.

A part of me knows that only through disillusion, through the certainty of failure and an absolute absence of hope, am I going to learn to burn as brightly as I'm determined to.

Argoitia is due back the day after tomorrow. Today I spent most of the time with my mom in her house in Tepoztlán.

Every time I see her, she gets a little older. I don't mean she's "gotten older," she gets older: it happens before my eyes, in a second, like a fruit wrinkling in a time-lapse sequence. What ages her is my gaze, and that's why I space out my visits now.

Mom realized I was in a strange mood and asked if something had happened with Argoitia, as if my maladies could arise only from that source. No, I said, it's something deeper: I've got nothing to say, or sometimes I do but it isn't a clear message, more like a noise, a sort of static that explodes in my ears, an electricity I've never been able to control. My mother was naturally alarmed by my reply. She asked if I was in therapy, if maybe it would do me good to talk to someone. I'm talking to you, I replied, and we left it at that.

I returned to Cuernavaca on a bus that dropped me at the downtown terminus and, as I was in the area, I decided to walk awhile before finding a cab to take me home. I passed Parque Revolución, the Centro Morelense de las Artes, and the Jardín Borda, then took a left to Plazuela del Zacate and stopped in front of the Palacio Cortés before walking around the Plaza de Armas and going for a "levantamuertos" juice in the Jardín Juárez. The sun was setting. The grackles in the plaza were making a deafening noise, drowning out any form of conversation. I finished my juice and walked back to the avenue to hail a cab. While I was waiting, I saw Erre coming out of the Cine Morelos. He looked pale, nervy, and was wearing a black shirt. He recognized me and stood stock still, his eyes wide open, as though he'd seen a ghost. I couldn't help but laugh.

Erre came up, looking like he was going to kiss my cheek, but I dodged and held out my hand. For the last months I've been trying to ensure I greet everyone that way: I'm sick of people rubbing their sweat into my skin, impregnating me with the smell of their invasive perfumes and aftershaves, and getting a close-up view of the corner of my mouth. Men generally take it badly, more so than women, but Erre thought I was just kidding and gave a sort of bow. At that moment, cars began to pass down the avenue—the traffic signals farther up had turned green—and I raised a hand to stop a cab. I got into the back seat and, with the door still open, raised my eyes to Erre's. Coming? I asked with as much seriousness as I could muster. Erre got in beside me and the cab headed off to a cacophony of horns. Santa María Ahuacatitlán, I told the driver; Erre looked at me in surprise. That's where I live now, I explained. With Martín Argoitia.

It's no big deal I said, but Erre's silence was tortured. He stared at the ceiling, hardly breathing, as if he wanted to vanish. It really isn't a big deal, I repeated, the whole story is funnier that way; it was fated. Erre put a hand to his jaw and half closed his eyes. I guessed he must have had a toothache or was pretending, inventing some ailment on the hoof to cover up his shame. And it really wasn't a big deal. Even while we were still in the cab, I knew it was a bad idea, that fucking with a former teenage sweetheart could only end badly. But Erre looked weak and lost, and I convinced myself that there was some form of equilibrium in it: meeting again after so many years outside the Cine Morelos, him at a disadvantage, sweating and in low spirits, with his black shirt, as out of place as a Dutchman in Africa.

Things flowed naturally at first. I paid for the cab, led him to the study, showed him my hiding place for the flask, and we took a few swigs of tequila, hoping to find the courage or the cool. We made a pretense of catching up for three minutes but it was obvious that we weren't there to talk about life. I made the first move. We kissed on the couch and pulled off each other's clothes. I wanted to laugh at the sight of his socks—very much the gentleman, I thought; a conservative gentleman who shops in Sanborns' menswear department—but I saved my comment for another moment so as not to spoil the mood. I was surprised to discover that Erre still smelled the same and that his body odor had been stored in some area of my subconscious all those years. I tried to move his hand between my legs, but from that instant things started to come to a standstill. The kisses and caresses were headed nowhere and I realized that his breathing had slowed slightly and he'd lost his hard-on. I tried stroking his dick to see if that would help but gave up after a while and sat beside him, our heads resting on the back of the couch. It's no big deal, I said. It really isn't a big deal.

Erre quickly dressed, hiding his limp penis. His shame gave me a warm feeling and then I was ashamed of that warmth; I guess I smiled, because he asked if I thought it was funny. A bit, I replied, teasing him. There was no point in trying to suppress my sense of humor: nothing was going to happen, anyway. He picked up the flask and swallowed the last shot. I have to go, he said, and I knew he was lying. He had nothing to do in Cuernavaca. Conejo had told me he was divorced, living with his parents, was forever complaining about ailments, and hadn't been able to chill out with him, even when they were smoking weed.

Okay, I said in a conciliatory tone, call me sometime and we'll have coffee. Erre stood there looking distracted and asked if I had any ibuprofen. I was slightly disconcerted by his question, the very different tone in his voice, as if he'd suddenly remembered something. I lazily put on my skirt and showed him to the bathroom. Argoitia had a pretty complete hoard of medicines in the cabinet over the basin. Take whatever you need, I said, and sat on the toilet lid. Erre read the labels, took a pill from three different packets, and swallowed them with a gulp of water from the faucet. I asked if he wanted me to call him a cab, but he told me he'd walk to the rank by the police station.

When we were at the gate, he moved closer again to kiss me goodbye and, once again, I backed off slightly and held out my hand. He didn't bow this time or offer his hand in return. Sorry, Natalia, I'm not in a good place right now, he said. Don't worry; it was good to see you, anyhow, I replied automatically, and it was only after I'd said those words that I realized they were true: against all the odds, and despite the awkwardness, I was a little pleased to have seen him.

I was pleased to see him back in Cuernavaca, divorced and downhearted, with erectile dysfunction; alone, sweaty, and out of place everywhere.

Erre clutched his jaw again, with the same expression of pain as before, and walked off down the cobbled street.

One of the bromeliads fell off the nail supporting it and in the fall broke its central calyx, which was about to flower. Not far off, I found some animal droppings—possibly the cacomixtle that lives in the untended area of the garden. I've attempted to save the bromeliad, but it's in bad shape. Plants don't fall with the same elegance as animals. There's no attempt to cushion the impact: they accept the embrace of the earth and yield unquestioningly to the whole debacle in a sordid kind of way.

My relationship with Argoitia has been more strained since his return. He's grumpier than usual, maybe because his tequila intake has increased. I have the feeling something happened in San Miguel de Allende. Most likely, he slept with another woman. I was once the lover he saw on the sly; it's not unlikely that it's my turn now to see things from the other side. Although it may be something else. Perhaps he didn't sleep with anyone and the issue is just his weight and the passing years; the intuition, ever more difficult to stifle, that he's wasted his time on the planet. His daughters scarcely talk to him. His exes can't bear the sight of him. Gallery owners treat him like an old dog that has to be tugged along during walks. Only government officials seek his company: hyenas who lick their lips at the veneer of prestige it brings to dine with the old oil painter. Argoitia isn't stupid. He's probably realized that his poor reputation among the younger generation is justified. He's weary. The speed of events seems to overtake him. He writes long-winded rants on Facebook about the banality of the world and his only likes are from the same sort of men and middle-aged women with high-up hairdos and low-level passions. There's a light inside Argoitia that sees everything: his decadence, the tepid warmth of my treatment of him, the certainty that the only person who takes him seriously is his cardiologist: that prophet of doom who urges him to change his lifestyle. Argoitia hides his fear behind a curtain of sarcasm and growls, but I know he knows; know he's going to die with the knowledge that he's made a lot of mistakes.

I've started working in the Jardín Borda, just to get away from the house, which seems to have been infected by the sinister aura of the overgrown part of the garden, where what remains of the fallen eucalyptus lies. I've been assigned a room in the Borda that I can use in the mornings on the pretext of holding auditions and rehearsing the piece. The surrounding park has been devastated by the drought: the plants are wilting and the fountains were turned off ages ago. I haven't yet felt like taking a look at the lakeside stage, but I've been told the lake is dry and full of trash. When our paths cross in the corridors, the director repeatedly tells me that they are sorting out a few problems there, but says everything will be ready for my performance; they are going to buy a tank of water. Just to worry him, I said there was no need to fill the lake: the drought-induced, gone-to-seed look fits better with the aesthetic I'm seeking.

The stories surrounding the garden bug me. Maximilian I of Mexico lived there, and at elementary school they beat that stuff about the imperial aura of Cuernavaca into us so soundly that I ended up detesting it, along with all the imagery of his wife, Carlota, the army uniforms designed by Maximilian himself, and so on and on. That and the overblown preeminence accorded to Alexander von Humboldt, given that he only ever spent a few hours in Cuernavaca before continuing on to Mexico City, and I find it unlikely that he, as legend goes, dubbed it "the city of eternal spring." I prefer the arid present: the eternal spring converted into a season of drought, the dry, barren garden, the streets scourged by dust, smoke, and the greed of those in power. There's no form of nostalgia worth exalting to an aesthetic value: any positive judgment about the past shows disdain for the present, a forgetting of the people here now, with us, hoping we'll look upon them with all the dignity we give to things now gone.

There were eighteen responses to my classified advertisement, if you include my friend Sonia, who did in fact attend a preliminary meeting at my invitation. The majority were women, but some of them persuaded their partners to come along—timid men who eyed one another nervously in embarrassment, as though ashamed to possess bodies. I interviewed the candidates separately to give the whole thing a professional air, but in fact I accepted them all. Six of them stepped down when they heard the details, either from fear of looking ridiculous or because they were expecting something more substantial in terms of pay (my budget, unwillingly handed over by the minister, is pretty much symbolic). There were, however, no complaints about the schedule: I told them there would be a couple of group sessions on weekends, but beyond that we could arrange things to suit their needs. Anyway, I'm also interested in working with them individually.

I arranged for them all to come to the room in the Jardín Borda the following weekend and booked a few individual sessions there for Wednesday afternoon.

Because of our past history, I made an exception for Sonia and decided to visit her at home on Tuesday to talk things through while her daughter crawled around us on the floor. When I outlined the piece to her, she laughed and told me I was crazy. Then she seemed to regret her reaction and hurriedly added that she loved the sound of the project. I know that's not true, that Sonia can't love the sound of it because she doesn't understand it, and this isn't going to be one of those pieces where the audience sighs, even though they don't know what's happening; it will be the kind where they get angry and ask for their money back.

•

One of my dancers is a fifty-seven-year-old woman named Amparo. I met her on Wednesday at 4:40 p.m. at a café on Calle Humboldt to talk about her role, ask a few questions, and show her some articles and sketches. (I want my dancers to conceive their parts alone to begin with, so they aren't thinking about what the others are doing.) Amparo took timid sips of her super-sweet coffee while I told her about the island of Blockula, the backwards movements, and the medieval choreomanias. I explained that I was interested in the dynamics of rumor and panic, the speed with which gossip ignites and burns whole hectares of countryside and cities. I also told her about Mary Wigman, her nervous breakdown, and her 1914 witch dance.

A strange light shone in Amparo's eyes. She dabbed her mouth with a napkin after each sip of her cappuccino, careful not to smudge her pink lipstick. At some point, I asked her what she thought, what movements came into her mind when I told her about Frau Troffea's contortions in the streets of Strasbourg. Instead of replying directly, she sat in silence, looking me straight in the eyes—something she'd avoided until then—and said, "When I was a child, one of my best friends disappeared from our school. She just stopped coming to class, and when we called her home, they hung up. We were thirteen or fourteen then, but the rumor was that she'd run off with her sweetheart, a boy who worked in the stationery store. None of the grown-ups mentioned it in front of us, nobody explained what had happened. One day we saw my friend's mother, all dressed in black, in the principal's office. Somebody said my friend was dead and everyone joined in the gossip. Some claimed her sweetheart had killed her, others that she'd died while giving birth to a weird baby, that she'd conceived some form of small animal. I particularly remember that last invention, because around that same time my father ran over a possum and I related the two events. Gradually, one rumor won out; my friend had killed herself because of a forbidden love: the boy in the stationery store came from a poor family and her parents didn't want them to go on seeing each other. We were at the age when you read a lot of novels, you know, and a romantic theory like that at least gave us the consolation that my friend had died for such a pure, intense form of love, like the ones you see on TV. After a few months, some other rumor started up, replacing the one about my friend, and everyone forgot about her. Except for me, naturally, because I missed her. I sometimes dreamed of her and would wake up in tears. In those dreams, my friend would tell me that she hadn't committed suicide, that she wasn't dead but in hiding. One afternoon, from the back seat of my father's car, I thought I saw her crossing the street in an area of the city we hardly ever passed through. I told the story at school the next day, but nobody took it seriously; they thought I'd invented it to attract attention. Some years later, when I was in college, I came across her working at a supermarket checkout. I asked her why she'd disappeared when we were kids and she told me that the boy in the stationery store had gotten her pregnant, but she'd lost the baby and her mom and dad had moved to another neighborhood and changed her school. I was still so innocent back then that I asked where she'd lost the baby. My friend burst out laughing and said she had to get back to work. I kept in touch with her and we began calling each other from time to time. After I got married, I lost track of her for a while, but one day her mother phoned me. My friend really had died this time and had left me an album of stickers we made together when we were young. I didn't know anyone at the vigil, but I eavesdropped on conversations and people were saying it was suicide. So, there you have it; years afterward, and for other reasons, the rumors going around the school had come true. Don't you think it's odd the way a rumor sometimes becomes a prophecy? What do you want us to wear for the performance? I've still got a dress in the closet from when I used to dance danzón with my husband, God rest his soul. I could wear it with black, mid-heel shoes."

Erre has tried to reestablish contact, sending me texts with ambiguous emojis (a wizard, a face with a monocle), as though that would pique my curiosity. I guess he's already forgotten the awkward episode in the study, or his sense of self-esteem has blocked it out and he's looking for a chance to redeem himself. Whatever, I haven't replied.

Conejo called to tell me another of his stories. This time he's convinced that the water in Cuernavaca is polluted with a new element called alfonsium, discovered by a scientist in Morelos State—Alfonso, or Poncho, Alberola—who has been gagged by the international community due to political interests. When I asked if he had any proof, he was evasive. The proof is all around us, he said, but if you don't want to see, there's no point in me showing it to you. He asked about my choreography and I told him that it was in good shape, but after the performance I'd have to look for somewhere else to live. Conejo gave a wicked laugh, like he did when we were teenagers and used to trash everyone in the world while eating oranges in the Arcadia schoolyard.

Thinking of the Arcadia reminded me of Erre. Before ending the call, I asked Conejo if he'd seen him again. His uneasy silence led me to deduce that not only had he seen him, but Erre had told him about our meeting. I don't know if he told the whole story. I don't think he would. He's too proud to admit to his best friend that he couldn't get it up.

When I hung up, I opened the door to the study and found Argoitia there, prowling nervously. He went to the kitchen, poured himself a shot of tequila, and said we needed to talk about something. At first, I thought he was finally going to tell me what happened in San Miguel de Allende: to confess his infidelities or excessive alcohol intake.

If that had been the case, I could have fessed up too and told him about Erre. When there's a balance in the cheating, a relationship has, without room for doubt, a future. But Argoitia wanted to know about my performance. The director of the Jardín Borda had seen me rehearsing with a dancer in the room I'd been assigned and was a little surprised that there weren't more people there. Instead of asking me directly, as anyone with an ounce of intelligence would, the cretin had rung Argoitia. I can imagine the conversation: My dear man, long time no see! How are your family? . . . Glad to hear it . . . The thing is that Señorita Natalia has been rehearsing, but with only one person . . . I just wanted to ask if it's going to be a small-scale event so I can organize a more suitable venue, the lakeside stage is pretty large and a single dancer would be lost there.

I brusquely informed him that I had no intention of discussing my piece in those terms, and said that if the director, or the minister, or the fucking municipal president was so concerned, he could talk to me instead of dragging in my partner, as if we were in school. Argoitia could tell he'd screwed up. You're right, my love, I won't get involved again, I'm absolutely certain your dance is going to be awesome, he said. And then he rounded off: I'll tell Bermúdez to talk to you himself when he sees you in the center.

After that failed intervention, Argoitia became more attentive. In the evening he put on bolero records and sang, clowning around while he cooked—it was the first time he'd done that since breaking his arm. The pasta was a bit overcooked and the sauce was too salty for me, but we had dinner on the terrace and opened a bottle of red wine that, according to him, he'd been saving for a long time. As far as I was concerned, it tasted like vinegar.

Today I had a plenary session with the interpreters of *The Great Noise*. I assembled them in the rehearsal room and read them fragments of Pascal Quignard's *L'Origine de la danse* as an introduction to an exercise: "For those guided by origin, their only goal in the movement they commence is nascent awkwardness . . . Beauty is linked to the awkwardness of origin."

After that, I projected a series of images onto one of the walls (it was almost impossible to get hold of a functioning projector: apparently the Ministry of Culture has only one and it was in the house of a pen pusher called Samuel: the unfathomable mysteries of bureaucracy). The first image I showed was a 1925 painting by the Argentinian artist Xul Solar called *San Danza*.

In the painting, three female characters, represented schematically, dance as if moving forward in the same direction, following a snake that seems to be standing upright on its tail and leaning on a cross. The first of the characters is carrying a placard or banner that springs from her head and has various symbols—incomprehensible hieroglyphs. The second woman, whose hair is in a ponytail, has one arm raised and the other pointing down as if she were imitating the stance of the first figure. The third woman's arms are the reverse of the others' (her left up and her right down in their case) and she also seems to be defecating as she dances. The three women are naked except for gold-colored anklets and tight collars, also golden, like the chokers worn a hundred years ago. I ask my dancers to comment on the painting, to say what they think of it, and after a few timid interventions, I give them more details about the artist and the work. A friend of Jorge Luis Borges, Xul Solar was a modern mystic who created his own language, Neocriollo, and worked with divinatory systems like the I Ching and the tarot. He was a follower of the great magus Aleister Crowley, on whose instigation he made a series of transcendental meditations and trance writings known as *San Signos*. This painting, *San Danza*, is in some way related to those hallucinatory experiences. The fact that the third woman is shitting as she dances suggests an altered state of consciousness, induced by a religious disposition, but also by the Bakhtinian notion of carnival, in which, through an inversion of values, base materials like shit can be considered sacred: the mythic conversion of shit to gold that obsessed so many anthropologists and not a few artists.

My dancers look at me in stupefaction and ask if they have to shit themselves ("soil themselves," they say) while they are dancing. I tell them that they don't *have to* do it but should be open to experiencing their bodies in an exceptional way during the performance.

A doubt-laden silence spreads through the group.

A Clear-Cut Vision

The epicenter of the pain seems to be in my jaw, but it's difficult to locate the exact spot: it could in fact be in my neck, or even my right temple. The pain has taken control, radiating like a sun in all directions, hiding its own point of origin. At times, it is a long file of ants heading upward from my back right molar to my forehead. At others, it's a river that runs from my ear to somewhere in my shoulder. It's like an electric storm, the sort where you can't tell if the lightning bolts are descending from the sky or sprouting from the earth: an instant of brilliance that blurs the boundaries of above and below. I can only ever forget about it for short periods, when I fix my eyes on a spot on the ceiling and give my imagination free rein, like a dog entering a gloomy forest without looking back.

The paint on the spot of the ceiling I stare at is patchy.

I've always seen different shapes there. When I was little, I'd look at it before going to sleep, before my parents switched off the light on the nightstand, and I'd clearly see a sort of mask. Later I started seeing two kneeling children, and since I found that image in a kind of daydream, I haven't seen the mask again. It's just like those optical illusions where you can see the profile of a young woman or the face of an old one. There's an irreversible click in perception, and suddenly it's impossible to escape the unambiguous image.

I clearly remember the moment, at the age of thirteen, when that click happened and the shape I saw in the blotch changed. I was staring at the mask when it disappeared, as if by magic; in its place were the two children, kneeling, possibly in prayer. Now that I've returned to my parents' home, when I spend hours staring at the blotch on the ceiling of what was my childhood bedroom, I can see only the little goatherds, as I call the figures.

As I said, looking at the blotch distracts me for a while, but when the pain returns after that break, it's with the strength of a falcon tightening its grip on the neck of a hare. A strength that doesn't wane until it has subdued, vanquished, neutralized its prey.

I look at the packet of ibuprofen on the nightstand by my bed. I have four 600 mg pills left. I could take one now to help me sleep and two more in the morning with breakfast. That way, I'll have one more for an emergency; it's a bad idea to run out of painkillers. Next to the packet is the notebook where I've been recording all my symptoms since the pains began a year ago. One day I'll show them to a generous, humanist doctor, who'll be able to decipher that apparent chaos;

who, in the luminous disorder of space, will see an unmistakable constellation.

It wasn't an easy night. I dreamed I was lost in the Jardín Borda—much bigger than it really is—and then suddenly I was standing in front of a sign saying, "This garden is for everyone, but only those with a clear-cut vision can enter." Then, in my dream, a stab of pain had me bent double, clutching my jaw, and I fell onto the roots of a tree—a rock fig.

I woke in a sweat, and in pain; it was still dark outside. I reached out a hand automatically for one of the pills, but the packet was empty. I didn't remember having taken the three remaining ibuprofen. The pain seemed to be moving from my jaw to my shoulder; that milky way once again, that asteroid belt of pain, a disaster zone.

I looked at my naked body in the bathroom mirror, only dimly illuminated by the light from the street filtering in through the branches of the African tulip tree—a warm amber glow that gave the bathroom, with its blue tiles from way back when, a sense of time having come to a standstill. I thought my shoulder looked red and swollen; or maybe that was just my perception, distorted by the pain, the darkness, the nightmare. I observed my body—at once familiar and foreign: the slight scar by my right eye (a childhood encounter with a glass tabletop); the curly pubic hair; the slightly jutting jaw. All of a sudden, I remembered that when I was twenty, I tried to make a movie short on a zero budget about identical twins who hated each other. How would it feel to hate someone who looks exactly like you?

I went back to bed, to my adolescent bed with its yellow metal tubes; I remember having chosen it when I was ten or eleven in a store near Plaza Cuernavaca. There are stickers for obscure punk bands on the yellow tubes; Conejo had given me them when we were in high school and I stuck them there to project a sort of gritty image. But the fact is that I've never liked those groups; the fact is that music is one of the many pleasures that have passed me by. I can listen for a while; at concerts I even sometimes become infected by the general excitement and jump up and down or pretend to know the words and join the chorus at the top of my lungs, but when I'm alone, with my headphones on, the bitter truth is unavoidable: music leaves me cold. Naturally, I've never told anyone; I know all too well that it's not the sort of defect you can confess to.

At the age of thirty-five, it felt ridiculous to be lying in that narrow, yellow bed covered in stickers. I switched on the lamp on the nightstand, but it was too bright so I turned it off again and stared at the screen of my phone until the sun came up. A chink of light peeked through a gap between the drapes and I watched it move across the floor; first touching one corner and then advancing to the middle of the room, slipping over a pair of socks lying there, and climbing up the legs of a chair until it merged with the ambient, less localized light. I looked at my phone again. It was seven o'clock.

Noises were coming from the kitchen and I went to see who was there. Mom was making coffee in her old moka pot; she wasn't wearing her glasses and that made her look fragile, sort of lost, like an animal during an eclipse. She smiled, as though surprised by my presence, and asked if I'd slept well. I guess she sometimes forgets that I'm here, that I've returned to her home and am spending my days in my yellow-tube, sticker-covered bed, staring at the blotch on the ceiling that looks like two little goatherds in prayer. We sat together at the table in the center of the kitchen, where my parents usually have breakfast and dinner when they eat at home. Neither of us said a word. There's nothing in the world more comfortable than the silence that fills a space when my mom is quiet.

After a while, the sound of the coffeepot broke the magic of that moment and Mom hurried over to pour. I refused the coffee she offered me and took a handful of ice cubes from the freezer, wrapped them in a dishrag, and put it on my shoulder. Is it still hurting? Mom asked, and without giving me a chance to reply added: It's stress. You'll see, it will be gone in a few weeks, now it's all over.

What's over, of course, is my marriage; my life, you might even say if you're given to exaggeration, but the truth is that my dramas are of a lower order: discreet pains that seem to have no end in sight, like that torture of the drip-drip of water drilling between your eyes.

The ice cubes have melted and the damp dishrag on the floor by my bed reminds me of the excitement of my first wet dreams—the sense that the most important thing in my life had, for the first time, happened at night, on the other side, the dark side. I decide to go to the pharmacy for ibuprofen: it's a mission no different from any other, an aim capable of getting me off my bed. I put on a black shirt, a pair of jeans, and the running shoes I've never worn for running. I look at myself again in the bathroom mirror and am irritated by my graceless appearance, my bloodshot eyes, the dried spittle at the corners of my mouth that I hastily rinse off.

As I'm passing the kitchen door, I see Mom and Dad having breakfast. An immutable image: the juice, the fruit, the steaming tortillas, the huevos a la mexicana on the plate. The institution of breakfast. Dad makes a comment about the fires, he says there's one that's been burning in almost the same spot for two weeks, as if the earth itself were alight. What can be left to burn? he asks, and I think that's a vaguely familiar metaphor for something, but I can't figure out what because I've had a bad night.

Then Dad's tone changes and he asks me if I'm going to have breakfast—I'm still standing by the door, watching them. No, I say, have to be off, stuff to do. At least take a banana with you, he says, but I'm already on my way; I open the street door, close it behind me, and turn to face the Cuernavaca sun, still not at its full strength.

Some horrendous residential buildings have been erected almost opposite the house: five identical fourteen-story towers with communal swimming pools and gardens, guards with menacing expressions, electric gates, and security cameras. Farther along the street, a new shopping mall has sprung up between two other malls, around three hundred meters from the mall that's been there since my adolescence. The neighborhood is unrecognizable—I'm unrecognizable, maybe my parents and the whole world are unrecognizable; there's no form of continuity, no causality, not even a correlation: there are voices, not people, the play of light and smoke, a lot of smoke blotting out the skies of Cuernavaca and the surrounding areas—but on the median strip in the avenue, I spot the drunk who's been reeling along these streets for the last fifteen years, if not longer. I'd almost swear he's still wearing the same filthy rags, the same disintegrating shoes, that he's carrying the same muddy gunny sack, like he's untouched by time. Maybe the poor dipso has always been here, laughing in the face of time like some god from before the separation of the earth and waters. Maybe he's the sole constant, the rock in the middle of the river that's wearing away too, but at a slower pace than us, who are tree trunks carried downriver by the current.

I decide not to cross the avenue, which would have meant a face-to-face encounter with the drunk: I don't want to recognize anything. As far as I'm concerned, they can build even more shopping malls, one on top of the other, like the cathedrals of warring religions, until there's nothing left of this parody of a city, nothing besides the sound of cash registers in the clouds of smoke.

Farther along, there's a café I don't recognize either. This is the city of my childhood, but it's also another city, in which I'm a tourist. I sit at a high table and order a double Turkish—it's apparently a Turkish café; the coffee takes forever to arrive and when it does it's sludgy. I drink it down in one, with a show of manliness, and wipe the dregs from my teeth with a napkin. I could read my future in the cup, but you can read the future any old time. It takes more courage not to: not to look into the bottomless depths of things in search of answers; to accept the impenetrable silence of the cup, its serene disdain.

But the temptation is too strong: I scrutinize the dregs. The coffee has created a landscape of dry riverbeds and valleys eroded by the wind. A barren planet. What can I extrapolate from that about my personal future? Nothing. I think of the blotch on the ceiling of my bedroom, its multiple forms. In comparison with all of this dumb stuff, that really is an eloquent blotch.

Then I look at the sky. A sky glimpsed beyond the clotted ash that obscures it. The clouds form landscapes that resemble those in the coffee dregs, on the ceiling: a fine, shifting gauze, an overflowing water source that later becomes a dry creek. Then the clouds and even the smoke partially clear and the sun finally comes out and, as I feared, heats the air. Cuernavaca at eleven in the morning.

Very soon, I think, there will be nothing left of this valley; when the fires have died down, high winds will blow in. Cuauhnáhuac, the "place by the trees," as the Nahuatl toponym describes it, will be an incomprehensible relic of the past, and the name the Conquistadores gave the city will, in the end, be its fate: *cuerna-vaca*, the horns of a cow, and sand, rock and sand, the skeletons of supermarkets scattered along a sandy valley. Parking lots, rust, saltpeter. Caracaras flying over the scrapyard in search of carrion.

I pay for the coffee and continue on my way. My steps lead me toward the former Casino de la Selva. More malls. The old Patios de la Estación, that in my day were home to an informal settlement—people living in abandoned railway cars, like nomads forced into a stationary lifestyle—now look like a theme park for something I can't quite put my finger on.

It's a long time since I've walked around this area. In the past, when I visited Mom and Dad, I'd drive from Mexico City, scarcely noticing my surroundings, and then I'd return, without making any stops en route, ignoring the existence of these streets, these people. But I can't be blamed for that blindness. I had a fairly full life: a car, a partner, a job that demanded my presence in the city at eight on Monday mornings. Now I'm in no hurry, I have no car, no other life to return to after this escapade, so I can continue my wanderings.

The Rutas, those recklessly driven, ancient microbuses, pack the streets, their horns sounding melodiously. There's a whole syntax of hooting that makes me feel like an ethnographer doing his level best to understand the rudiments of a language. The drivers shout abuse or spit out the window. There's always someone hanging out the back door, announcing destinations and collecting fares, like a Charon in a Club America T-shirt. I decide to take the pedestrian bridge across the avenue, but once on the steps up, pain shoots through me like a poisoned arrow; my right shoulder, or my neck: again, that vague heat, that black hole in some imprecise place, sucking away my life. Yes, that's it: an alien bloodsucker that attaches itself to my trapezius muscle and absorbs my energy as it electrocutes me.

High up on the bridge, I squint my eyes, searching for a pharmacy. I'm sweating. Wearing the black shirt was a bad decision. In the last two years or so, all my decisions have been pretty bad. Sweat is running down one side of my torso, down my arm, as if tracing out possible routes of pain, scouting the terrain of my body so it will later hurt, smolder, burn, tremble, and swell under the effects of who knows what force.

The Instituto Arcadia was around here, two hundred meters farther down, but it no longer exists. I used to walk this route to school every morning to meet Conejo and Natalia at the tables in the cafeteria before cutting class to go downtown or to Conejo's house, or to the trout farm in the gully near Santa María Ahuacatitlán. But in reality, it wasn't me who used to hang out in this neighborhood, but someone else; some other moment, some other world, some other city, and some other body. Nothing remains of that era.

I walk to the area known as El Túnel to cross one of the city's seven intersecting ravines and then continue uphill, along Avenida Morelos. I need to see Conejo.

I wake in pain during the night, lying in the yellow-tube bed. I remember practically nothing about yesterday, except for Conejo's bursts of laughter, Señor Bertini's white cane by the door of his office, a conversation about contaminated water and brainwashing. Then walking back to my parents' house along streets with no sidewalks. But I don't know what happened after that, if I had dinner, or what time I turned in.

I don't want to think about her, about my ex-wife. I don't want to think of her name and use that horrible term *ex-wife* simply as a means of imposing a distance, of saving myself from a memory that's threatening to exacerbate all my pains. There are words like that, words that don't signal or refer, but separate and protect you—from reality, its craggy zones—and are used to avoid saying a name, to avoid giving voice, body, face, and emotion to the tight knot in your throat.

But there are times, like now, when I trip up: I say "Lucía" in the night, barely voicing the three syllables. Lu-cí-a, like a spell that can send me to hell all over again.

I slept on my left side, turning my back to the outside wall, to the world. As a consequence, my left shoulder is exploding, throbbing with pain. Was it my left side that hurt yesterday, that will hurt tomorrow? I consult the blotch on the ceiling and the notebook where I sometimes make telegraphic jottings about symptoms. I can't remember, he can't remember: the last entry is from days ago and is only "hand, elbow, legs." Who wrote that?

Maybe the pain is running through my body systematically, making a detailed inventory of what I am, of what's still alive in me. I feel as though someone operated on me while I was asleep, cutting into my skin and then the muscle with a scalpel right to the center of the joint; it's like someone, that midnight surgeon, put a pellet—maybe made of steel—in the center of the joint, or perhaps a stone, a porous pebble; like someone then sutured the wound, neatly, almost with loving care, sewing my muscle and skin, leaving no trace. Now, in my left shoulder, I have a piece of volcanic rock, a lunar stone that scrapes, chips, messes up, and destroys the internal tissues of my arm at the least movement. I feel my arm and it's hot.

I try turning over to sleep on my other side, on my right arm, but can't get comfortable. Then I try sleeping on my front, on my back, I try propping myself up on an extra pillow, but nothing works. With each new position, another nuance of the same pain surfaces, reveals itself.

The predominant sensation is that my body is crushing me—or crushing itself, I don't know how to put it. If I lie on my left side, gravity plagues the painful arm: the whole mass of my body presses down on, crushes, compresses my arm and my side, and even my left hip and leg, plus my left knee, and my jaw too. If I turn onto my right side, it's the same: the natural force with which the earth attracts all bodies in my case becomes a destructive, or at least—let's not exaggerate—uncomfortable force. Lying on my back, I feel the mere weight of my chest—its contents: the heart, lungs, digestive tract; but also the things I resent and repent—is hurting and damaging my spine. And it seems like the total mass of my head, including the almost liquid mass of my eyeballs, is weighing on my neck, wearing it down, annihilating it.

The only places I'd be able to really sleep are in a zero-gravity simulator, or in space. I'd sleep like a baby in a spacecraft, free from all attachments, suspended in the air, in the center of the vessel. Or in a sensory deprivation chamber, in a tank filled with salt water that would allow me to experience that void, that extreme lightness that gravity and surfaces snatch from me.

There was a time, in another life, when on special occasions I used to go to a spa on Paseo de la Reforma in Mexico City to spend an hour floating in one of those salt-water tanks. In there, everything was dark and silent, and when I closed my eyes, my memories and future expectations would get mixed up and mingle—a miasma of nonlinear, stagnating time that I'd contemplate with the placid distance of the angels. I was obsessed with that apparently simple therapy, capable of reigniting a spark of enthusiasm for life. I found out as much as I could about the inventor of those tanks, a sort of mad scientist named John C. Lilly, who devoted his life to exploring psychoactive drugs and interspecies communication: he wrote papers on the language of dolphins, took high doses of LSD while swimming with them, and invented that form of fetal, suspended meditation that has become known as the sensory deprivation tank. But the twentieth century's talent for converting any invention into a weapon of war played against him: the CIA appropriated his theories and used them in interrogations. They put dissidents in those tanks after giving them dangerously high doses of LSD and forced them to float in the salty water until their skin dried out and cracked, with a background of bad-tripping music that was paused only for questioning. Sensory deprivation chambers, initially designed as an aid to transcendental meditation and consciousness expansion, became a form of torture that was later used in MKUltra, the infamous mental control program the United States government set up during the sixties.

I don't know how John C. Lilly felt about this violent reading of his pacific contribution to the new-age world, but I suspect he didn't like it much. Perhaps he would have preferred to know that, in contrast, decades later, a Mexican man would find a moment of solace in the artificial womb of the tank while his life was on a slow descent into disaster.

But I don't have the money for things like that these days. I don't have any money, period: the last few thousand pesos of my severance pay and savings went to the divorce lawyer's fee and the three months' rent I owed to my landlady.

Defeated, I sit on a corner of the bed and check the time on the overly bright screen of my phone. Four in the morning. I look again: five. I blink: it's six, the sun is about to—threatening to—come up, it's nearly daytime and the lacerating gravity of night retreats a little, allowing me to see things in the light of reason and breakfast. I get up and go to the bathroom. My throat is clogged with a kind of thick phlegm; it hurts to swallow. After a few minutes standing at the sink, I manage to cough up a dark gob: the fine ash that, I think, is gradually blocking my respiratory tract. Though maybe it's just dust.

My feet hurt almost as much as my shoulder did earlier. The weight of my whole body, exercising perpendicular pressure on the soles, is close to unbearable. For a moment I think I can feel a lump in my instep, as though something inside my foot has broken and, having slipped out of place, is visible beneath the soft surface of my sleeping skin. Maybe walking all the way to Conejo's and back yesterday was too much. I'm not used to Cuernavaca's steep slopes any longer, to the cobbled downtown streets, the pedestrian footbridges with loose metal rails and the steps in lousy condition.

I've started the day on the wrong foot.

Still defeated, I sit on the edge of the bed again, my elbows on my knees, chin resting in my palms. I stare at my feet. Something does in fact seem to be out of place in them. They're someone else's feet, someone who's lived two or three years longer than me—those bad years when every day is like a lizard trying to cross the highway, moving very slowly, always in danger of becoming roadkill. In the shadows of my bedroom—in the six, nearly seven o'clock shadows, with light filtering through the branches of the old tulip tree—they suddenly feel like the feet of an old man, the very old man I'll be if I make it that far: the anticipated future I'd prefer not to glimpse in the early hours (I look at my clock: it's seven), in the light of day.

Somewhere in the distance, I can hear voices; possibly two drunks walking along the street or a couple having an argument in a garden four or five houses away. A fair amount of the private life of this neighborhood takes place in gardens. Among the bougainvillea, children experience the first flush of sexual attraction; by a guava tree, youths embrace and sway, lulled by alcohol and taco binges; old folk contemplate the flower of the cacaloxóchitl when it opens in early May and then, in the blink of an eye, it's late August and they're watching the tree shed its bark. From one garden to another you can hear, you might even say breathe, all that living outflow, that constant bustle of births, dances, and deaths.

Projected onto the curtains, the shadow of the African tulip tree is a ghostly, but at least familiar presence. I remember that when I was small, I enjoyed playing with its dry seedpods, which were like small boats. I'd fill a washbowl with water from the hosepipe in the garden and float the pods in it; I re-created naval battles and shipwrecks, telling the stories of tragedies in that verb tense used only in games that could be called the *ludic past*: "and then I was sinking and my boat was going down to the seabed with me." And then I was sinking.

I dress slowly (a black shirt again, the same one: I wear a bad decision like someone hanging a medal around their neck) and leave the bedroom. I walk down the short but dark hallway to the kitchen, where my father offers me a dish of papaya, Mom asks if my shoulder is still hurting, and I ignore them, say goodbye, and go outside again into the gross sunlight, the smoke-laden air to have a Turkish coffee as sludgy as the future of this beleaguered city studded with supermarkets.

I automatically head through El Túnel toward downtown. Just like yesterday, the same route. I need to visit Conejo, I think.

I've lived this day before and will maybe live it again in the future. While the world is coming to an end, it's important—supremely important—to get into a routine. Cling to a set of rituals, familiar paths, people we can return to in order to recognize ourselves.

Cuernavaca has the appearance of a chain of parking lots: I could cross the whole city, walking from one lot to the next under the blazing sun. In each of them, the same elderly man asks if you can spare some small change and offers to load your supermarket bags into the trunk of the car; the same menacing SUV with tinted windows, whose driver is a narco, a Chilango, or a suburban mom arriving to have her nails done before going for coffee.

I make an attempt to reconstruct the route I took yesterday. To walk along the same streets with no sidewalks and pass the same stinking ravines to reach Tlaltenango, but I don't remember if I really did walk here or if it's a false memory. In addition, the pain in my left shoulder, which sometimes extends to my neck and jaw, makes any form of intellectual exercise, however minimal, impossible. Just why did I put on this black shirt? The smell betrays that idiotic repetition—and forebodes others.

•

The street where Conejo lives brings back memories of more kindly days, when we were studying together at the Arcadia and used to spend a lot of time in his room, lying side by side on the gray rug, our feet on his bed, our blood flowing to our heads, chatting about nothing in particular, imagining futures that were always happier than the long-drawn-out finale in which we now live, plagued by wildfires, shootouts, and thinly veiled totalitarianisms. We'd smoke as we lay there, and the hours would pass, and instead of going to school, we'd stare at the ceiling—just as I stare at the ceiling at night now, in my parents' home, seeking the blotch that had a different, now forgotten shape; we'd stare at the ceiling and fantasize about going to South America—only rich kids and fools go to Europe—when we finished high school; about meeting men and women and kissing them all and sampling hallucinogenic roots from the Amazonas in a ritual context and, just maybe, finding work in some dream city like Buenos Aires or Rio, where we'd succeed in making our adult lives into a series of epiphanies. Then Conejo's father—Señor Bertini, who hadn't yet gone blind, but was seriously shortsighted—would come in to ask why we weren't at school or doing something productive, but there would be no need to reply because, however hard we tried, there was no satisfactory answer: we were there because we knew how to be totally in a place, the way stones are; like dogs lying motionless in the sun until nightfall beside the dried-out tortillas on the sidewalks of small towns with dirt streets, their eyelids drooping, until evening falls; like children getting sunburned in summer, playing in vacant lots and going back home after dark with their necks on fire and the sense of having spent a whole life wrapped up in games and arguments that seem—are—more important than life itself (more important than the news, homework, chila wasp stings, and even more important than eating). That was us. Two teenagers lying on a rug who had unintentionally disproved Copernicus, because the center of the known universe was that room, that light, Conejo's booming laugh as he told, for the umpteenth time, the story of some ridiculous event in the Arcadia (one of the teachers invited two Freemasons to speak to us about the history of their lodges in Mexico; a fellow student who set fire to a desk). That was us, and that house, to which I'm now headed on the shady side of the street, was where we could be those people, shutting our eyes to all the wars; a small yellow-painted house (there was more yellow about back then; now it's close to being an extinct color), in which, in addition to Señor Bertini, lived Señora Bertini—Conejo's mother—who later left her husband for his ophthalmologist (the son of a bitch of an ophthalmologist who never managed to slow the advance of Señor Bertini's condition, leaving him at once blind and single). And in that house—to which I'm headed, sweaty and hurting, wearing my stinking black shirt—our friendship was forged, and Natalia also entered the circle of that conflict-proof complicity that has only faded with time, as does everything.

I ring the doorbell.

Since my return to Cuernavaca, I've been constantly thinking about running into her; Natalia, that is. I remember other chance meetings, years ago: once when we came across each other mid-morning in the park behind the bus terminal; another time—mid-afternoon—I spotted her racing down one of those long, steep streets in the Club de Golf neighborhood, and followed her stealthily, running and hiding behind parked vehicles until we reached a vacant lot overlooking a ravine and, on the opposite slope, a huddle of tin shacks. On that kind of lookout point, from which you can see both the craggy orography of the city, with its greenish waterways, and the sad poverty of its inhabitants, I went up to Natalia and told her I'd been following her for quite a few blocks, and she said she knew, said I was always following her like a slave, and we laughed and pushed each other as if picking a fight and then got entangled in an inexpert, hot kiss until our teeth clashed and we moved apart in embarrassment.

That whole sequence was typical of the period when we were dating: a chase, the pantomime of a brawl, gauche, suppressed desire, and then a step back, like a hand pulling away on contact with a hot pan. But we didn't know any better because that was the era of first times, so we loved, desired each other in an erratic, syncopated way, and later we'd catch each other's eye in class and believe for an instant in telepathy.

At other times, we'd cut class and, with a conspiratorial air, the three of us would end up in Conejo's bedroom listening to music or pretending to like beer until Señor Bertini came back from work and kicked us out, shouting: Go home and study, you slackers! Or you'll end up like your friend—pointing to Conejo—with his gangster haircut. But they were kindly reprimands, with a hint of parody. Señor Bertini was a former Communist who had become disillusioned with activism but wouldn't have had a moment's doubt in taking up arms if Conejo had asked: he was so susceptible to his son's blackmail, and in such a heartwarming way, that Conejo found it almost painful. That may be why he tormented his father: like when he was fifteen, and disappeared from a camp near Huitzilac without telling anyone to spend the night in the forest; or when he created a furor in high school by turning up stoned, or the time he decided to become a Hare Krishna for two weeks.

Later, when his mom—who had always been pretty much absent—ran off with the ophthalmologist, Conejo moderated his rebellious spirit and began looking after his increasingly debilitated father, resigned to his fate but also with kindness.

When our small group disbanded, Natalia continued to see Conejo on her own but that holy trinity, in which we rehearsed the roles we'd have to play in the awful adult world, never re-formed.

The sky is a crazy mix of colors, like a rotting orange. In the Jardín Juárez, the grackles sound off at all hours. I'm not sure if I'm inventing the despair I detect in their squawks. I order a mamey sapote smoothie at the kiosk and smile as I remember that years ago there was a rumor that the run-down kiosk where they sell juice and smoothies was, like the tower that bears his name, the work of Gustave Eiffel. In no time at all, the garden filled with impromptu tourist guides who offered detailed accounts of how the kiosk donated by Monsieur Eiffel was brought (suspended from a Zeppelin according to some versions) to the Heroic City of Cuernavaca, the apple of his eye. Where did that story originate? There's no way to weed out the legends, fantasies, and downright lies from history, I think, as I walk to the Plaza de Armas.

In spite of the wildfires, in spite of the authorities warning against open-air activities, the streets are quite crowded, there's a lot of movement. Suddenly, as if emerging from the smoke, a woman appears wearing a face mask with a design like the teeth of a calavera. I watch her as she walks toward me and she returns my gaze—my stares—before moving past and disappearing into the throng. Every day is the Day of the Dead.

In the Zócalo, a huge evangelical service is being held with permission from the mayor, who long ago betrayed the much-vaunted state policy of laicism. The congregation is obviously not well off. They're wearing their best clothes for the ceremony: threadbare jackets and blouses buttoned up to the neck, with barely perceptible sweat marks in the armpits. Large families; kids dragged along by one arm by the brute force of a mother in a hurry, trying to shove her way through to get a better view of Don Profeta—the famous Cuernavaca pastor from the poor La Barona neighborhood.

The sound system is better than that of any concert I've attended. Don Profeta's voice comes across loud and clear from the stage on which he's yelling to the farthest corners of the square and even the surrounding streets leading to the Mercado Santos Degollado. The rapt congregation nods automatically at each of his assertions and adds a spontaneous *Amen* to the most impassioned.

I make an effort to focus on his words, but it's an emotional speech, almost in code, with allusions to the flames of hell and a group of chosen people to whom, I assume, I'll never belong due to everything I've done and intend to go on doing, as far as my pain will allow.

A small boy is pissing against a tree in one of the planters on the edge of the square while his mother listens engrossed to the sermon; Don Profeta is now asking God to send rain to put an end to the fires and the dry season. The crowd accompanies him in a prayer that sounds to me like the buzzing of bees.

Dusk is finally descending. It's been a long day, or a chain of several days without a night in between; days of walking aimlessly, nights of waking in pain and staring at the ceiling, days and nights mixed up together, and parking lots without a beginning or end, under a sun that tinges the atmosphere a weird shade—washed-out yellow.

The pain in my jaw returns, but on the right side now. And then a stabbing sensation in the sole of my left foot. There's something not right in my body, something moving out of place and displacing me.

I head south along Avenida Juárez. The noise of the grackles continues, even though it's almost completely dark by now. Palm trees sway in the wind and I think that maybe, with a little luck, the air currents will carry the smoke to the south of the state, where there are fewer gullies for it to get trapped in, and so give our lungs a break.

I haven't slept well for nights, waking in the early hours to spy on the slow mutations of the blotch on the ceiling. My eyes feel heavy, but I have a destination, a possible stopping-off point to slow down the world: Conejo has given me the name of a man who can get me any medication I want. Probably a doctor with debts who's trying to supplement his income by dealing on the side. I don't know how Conejo found out about him; even though he appears to spend the whole day in isolation at home, he actually has a lot of resources and friends.

The bell for the doctor's office, to one side of a large, black door, is labeled Dr. Rufino Bremen. Conejo had explained that he goes by the name of Miranda, apparently because he's concerned for his safety, yet here's a plaque with his real name. I find it calming to know that his lack of experience in trafficking drugs is on a level with mine in buying them.

His office is on the second floor of a building with a pizzeria at ground level; the pizzeria is empty, but the music—instrumental cumbia with a strong bass line that sounds to me Peruvian—blasts out in the hope of attracting customers. I ring the bell and glance up in case someone appears on the balcony, but instead of looking there, I fix my eyes on the stationary, grayish clouds, that dense, clotted substance that's been floating over a sizable area of central Mexico for weeks.

Dr. Rufino—or Miranda, or Bremen—opens the door and asks me to follow him up a metal spiral staircase. It turns out that his office is also his apartment: there are dirty plates on a table, a sofa bed with a throw, and a small consulting area that can be partitioned off. Beyond the glass door to the narrow balcony are three moribund plants and one of those old ashtrays that look like pieces of furniture, full of cigarette butts. And beyond that the palm trees on the median strip of Avenida Juárez.

To make small talk, I ask the doctor about his specialty, but he gives me a reproving look and in turn asks what the hell I want. Straight out, without any preamble. He seems nervous, lights a cigarette and smokes it as though it were his last, as though he were about to step, weak-kneed, onto a wooden scaffold in a public square. A strong analgesic, I reply. My shoulder and jaw are very painful, and something different hurts every day; it's a weird pain, like something is growing inside me, in my joints; a pain that's smoldering in the background and makes my skin slightly red. Dr. Miranda, Dr. Rufino, isn't listening: he's looking at the amber tip of his cigarette. I return to the main point, to the only point it's important to get across to him: I want something strong, very strong, for pain. Ketorolac isn't working anymore, and the same goes for anything I can buy over the counter.

The doctor disappears behind the screen that forms a poor partition between his home and his office and leaves me standing by the window. I look at the streetlamps, which illuminate the surrounding smoke, and think that it's a long time since we've seen any flies, moths, or beetles. In my childhood, Cuernavaca was a city full of insects. At night, bugs were always flying around the streetlamps with bats flitting by to gobble them up. In summer there would be mayates, lovable beetles that allowed themselves to be handled by the local kids. (We'd tie their feet with a long cord attached to our hands, and the beetles would fly in circles, like kites.) And, just before the rains began, the schoolyard would be overrun by leafcutter ants: a large-headed species that we used to make fight until they tore each other to pieces—we bet marzipan cookies on the outcome. And there were also honeybees, bumblebees, chila wasps; all sipping the nectar of the may flowers, sniffing the rotting scent of the tulip tree blossom, or messing with the hallucinogenic properties of the angel's trumpet flower, which would open for them. Nowadays there's only the nonstop noise of grackles, the smoke from the wildfires, and evangelists.

Dr. Rufino—or Bremen, or Miranda—hands me a small white plastic bottle, identical to every other container of medication, with the seal broken and the instructions for use in very small letters: Permutal 15 mg, not to be taken during pregnancy or breastfeeding, keep out of the reach of . . . The bottle isn't full, but there must be about twenty left, he says.

When you've finished these, come back, or try tramadol. You can buy that over the counter. How much do I owe you, Doctor? I ask, and for a moment wonder if that "doctor" is going a bit too far: but then he is one, as well as being a dealer. What's the correct form of address in such a case? Let's call it a thousand, he replies.

That feels expensive, very expensive, but I'm not in any mood to haggle. I shake the bottle to hear the sound the pills make, then I put it in my pocket and take out my wallet. As I hand over the cash, I ask the doctor how many pills I should take. Season to taste, he replies with a smile, and after a pause adds: But don't go knocking back more than five at a time. Start with two taken orally, or if you want a quicker hit, grind them and snort. Then just take it from there.

The loud cumbia from downstairs fills the office along with the aroma of oven-baked pizza and poor-quality, burned cheese, which mingles with the smell of the air, the smell of revoltingly murky ether that has flooded the city and the surrounding areas.

Outside in the street, I hail a cab and give Conejo's address. I don't feel up to having dinner with my parents. I send Mom a text telling her not to wait, to eat without me; it feels odd to have to start sending messages like that at the age of thirty-five.

On the way to Conejo's, I analyze the contents of the bottle. Twenty pills. I take one, swallowing it dry. The taste of medication lingers on my tongue, in my throat; a thick, cloying, bitter vestige.

Just for a moment, imagine it's true, says Conejo. Imagine the water in Cuernavaca is contaminated with a poisonous chemical nobody else has managed to identify. I look skeptical and reply that it would have no effect on our health; no one here drinks straight from the faucet. And if they did, I add, the presence of fecal matter in the water is more likely to make you sick than some magical substance nobody else knows about.

Conejo looks at me suspiciously. What do you mean, it would have no effect? Haven't you heard that in communities with a slightly higher than normal level of lithium in the drinking water, there's a lower incidence of suicides? And lithium is an element, just like alfonsium. It's just that alfonsium has other effects: it turns people evangelical.

I can never figure out if he really believes the things he

says he believes in, or if he's just killing time, or gets pumped up by fake news the way other people do about sport. He reels off information that not even the most poorly informed of my aunts and uncles would dream of repeating in a co-op group chat, and for Conejo it's all true, with no room for doubt: truth is a state of mind, a lifestyle choice. You only have to put a name to something for truth to gloriously burst in like an archangel descending over the most disturbing materials, over shit.

His bedroom is almost the same as when we were in our teens, and so are his clothes. He's still wearing the T-shirts of obscure bands, torn jeans, and knockoff Converse sneakers. But now he's a grown man who's going bald at the speed of light, and I'm a grown man with chronic pain and one divorce under my belt; here we are, sitting in his bedroom like we did twenty years ago, talking about nothing, pretending that there's a sky outside, for now.

Conejo's books are scattered around the floor, some of them open facedown, like he'd left them that way so he didn't lose his page. They're mostly science fiction, although he does have some popular science books from the Fondo de Cultura Económica's Brevarios series: small, beat-up copies you can hardly even find these days. He tells me that he buys them in a place called Súper Libros, run by a Chilean man who fled the Pinochet regime and ended up here; he has a bookstore in Plaza Cuernavaca, over a Banamex and next door to a stationery outlet called La Michocana. The Chilean can get him any title he wants. Another of those connections Conejo's so proud of.

He has this fantasy of becoming a popular science author,

or more specifically writing about scientific phenomena nobody thinks are real. That's the opposite of science, I comment, and Conejo laughs. He tells me a convoluted story about intestinal bacteria and their relationship to autism.

It suddenly dawns on me that Conejo is getting more and more like his father, or at least the version of his father I remember from our teenage years, before he lost his sight. Señor Bertini was always telling stories. Conejo and I would come home from a party at three in the morning, and his father would be leaning on the kitchen counter, drinking black coffee, waiting to tell us that in 1941 a group of Nazis attacked Pablo Neruda in the restaurant of the Hotel Alemán, in the center of the city; or that in 1979 he and a friend went to a house in Calle Humboldt because they had been told that the legendary jazz musician Charles Mingus lived there, but the woman who came to the door said Mingus had died the night before.

These days, Señor Bertini shares his knowledge less often, but Conejo seems to have finally taken those Cuernavaca stories we grew up with seriously and has picked up the baton. Naturally, in his case the real story inevitably gets mixed up with the most nonsensical fabrications. Like that stuff about the water from the faucet being contaminated by a poisonous metal that doesn't appear in the periodic table.

Among the books and trash strewn on the bedroom floor, there's also a smallish pink dildo. Conejo notices that I'm eyeing it and explains, without the least embarrassment, that it's clean so I don't need to worry. We should buy you one, Erre. The way you look, it's clear as daylight you need to stick things up your ass. You must have one of the tightest asses in the universe, that's why you have so many aches and pains. Just get yourself a butt plug, lie on that silly little bed in your mom and dad's house, and put it in slow, little by little, so it doesn't hurt. If your mom calls you, just say you're busy and will wash the dishes later. I give his thigh a gentle punch, Conejo emits his stupid laugh and goes on: There's no need to jerk off or any of that, just loosening up a little is enough. You leave it there for a while and breathe. And afterward you'll feel way more relaxed, less bottled-up. You can't go through life being such an anal-retentive bastard. And it might even get rid of your ailments without fucking up your liver with those pills.

The mention of a remedy seems to bring on the pain. An electric current shoots through my shoulder again, as though an invisible hand were bunching up my nerve endings and squeezing them tight. My groan of pain doesn't go unnoticed and Conejo asks if the medication has kicked in. No, not yet, I think I'll take another pill. Then I remember Dr. Rufino's advice and decide to grind one on a book I pick up from the floor (J. G. Ballard's *The Unlimited Dream Company*). With the book on my lap and a twenty-peso bill rolled to form a straw, I inhale the white powder and fall back onto my friend's bed, like someone in a scene from a movie about drug addicts. But I'm only seeking pain relief.

I wake during the night, in pain, lying in the yellow-tube bed. I float in the darkness of my bedroom as though it were a sensory deprivation tank, wondering if what I'm doing is meditation or torture, consciousness raising or scratching the sores of my guilty conscience, inner illumination or self-inflicted grilling. "Isolated in the inner domains," writes John C. Lilly about his chambers, "the observer-agent can transform into, be transformed into any form." I close my eyes and try to change myself into an African tulip tree, like the one outside my window, but, predictably, it doesn't work.

I don't want to think about her.

For an instant I think I hear rain outside, but it's only the wind. For the last week dust devils have blown up overnight, fanning the flames of the wildfires in the forests and filling the city with ash and garbage. In the mornings, pools in the richer neighborhoods are filled with dirt and dry leaves; sickly trees, brought down by the strong winds, fall into the streets with no sidewalks.

I think about my life six months ago: a covertly endangered ordinariness, like a wooden table whose termite-infested legs are about to crumple under its own weight. I don't want to think about her, my ex-wife: the way she handled the car on the highway with the confidence of a racing driver; the nightstand at her side of the bed, always piled with books that she sometimes attempted to explain to me before switching off the lights. I don't want to speak her name, but, once again, I relapse: Lucía. And when I say it, I also remember that other person I was while I was with her: a likable, smart kind of guy with no pain, who made breakfast every morning because she always slept in. The kind of guy who doesn't know his own luck.

I look at my phone but forget to check the time and instead scroll through the news and my social media. For the last few days, information has been posted about the wildfires and their health effects. All sorts of information: advice, official bulletins, rumors, infographics, memes. Graphs explaining the damage to the lungs caused by inhalation of PM 2.5 particles, stories of strange phenomena in certain towns, reports of people passing out from smoke inhalation. Anyone who can has left for Mexico City, where, paradoxically, the air is cleaner, or for the Guerrero coast, beyond the officially designated emergency zone. But escape isn't easy either. There are fresh reports every day of highways closed due to the heat of ongoing fires; cars breaking down when ash gets in their engines. There's no way of knowing which reports are true and which are exaggerations, or just plain inventions spontaneously thought up by the collective.

In the streets of Cuernavaca, the sense of something abnormal in the climate is heightened by the open-air evangelical services with top-quality production values. Heat seems to be issuing straight from the asphalt, but there are also dust storms in the evenings, when the wind is cooler, even if it still causes damage.

Dad invited me to have coffee this morning. He's been overweight for the last few years—it's a taboo subject: he himself is the elephant in the room nobody mentions—and sweats like someone on death row in the desert. The perspiration streaming down from his armpits makes his checkered Costco shirt stick to his sides.

We left the house on foot; in the distance, I spotted the vagrant who's always hanging around here and considered saying something about him to my father, but then I thought he probably didn't even see the man, as if he's a personalized mirage, materializing for my eyes alone each time I leave the house.

We walked for forty meters along the sidewalk and, when I turned to look, my father was panting and sweating like he'd just run the Mexicali marathon. He said he wanted to go back home and take the car, which has AC.

Once in the vehicle, he waited for his breathing to return to normal and, before setting off again, asked what I was intending to do with my life now. His expression was grave, and I understood that he wanted to have a real man-to-man talk with me. I felt a twinge in my jaw and regretted not having taken an extra pill before leaving home. The AC smelled dusty (my father rarely drives, he hardly ever goes out). It might be worse than breathing the polluted air outside, those damned suspended particles.

I don't know what I intend to do with my life now, I tell him, repeating his words with ironic emphasis. I guess I'll stay in Cuernavaca for a few months before returning to D.F. to look for a job. (When I'm with him, I still call Mexico City the Distrito Federal because my father hates the change of name.) Or I might look for something to do here and stay longer, I added after a pause. He made no reply, just continued cruising with no fixed destination, his eyes half closed, the sweat now drying on his forehead. We entered a residential neighborhood with steep inclines and large, empty houses whose owners—I hypothesized—had escaped to Houston or the Caribbean. My father was accelerating and then braking abruptly at each intersection, as if someone were chasing us, as if he were lost in a city where he's lived his whole life. Where are you headed? I asked nervously. Don't know, he admitted in a defeated tone. And with a sadness that seemed to come from somewhere very deep inside, he added: Let's go back home, I don't feel like doing anything. To save the situation, it occurred to me to ask him to drop me off downtown on his way. You shouldn't spend so much time outdoors in all that smoke, he said, but began driving toward the center, finally having a destination in mind. He looked relieved. Although he hadn't managed to have a real man-to-man talk with me or make me reflect on the course my life was taking, he was at least driving in some fixed direction, and he clung to that direction as he did to his pension and his marriage.

•

Things hadn't always been that way. My father used to have long periods of proverbial lightheartedness, of unbounded optimism. He was a cheerful, loving father when I was little. (The whole family predicted great things for me, and it never entered their heads to think that brilliant future would slip through my hands as naturally as it did.) From the age of ten, he used to encourage me to take any extracurricular class that occurred to me, and he himself went through a stage of sport fads that he channeled into such areas as mountain climbing or adventure tourism.

Once, when I was twelve, Dad decided that we weren't spending enough time together and organized a camping trip, just for the two of us, over a long weekend or a short school vacation. The week before we were due to go was dedicated to preparations: we went to Plaza Cuernavaca to buy a tent, two sleeping bags, a thermos, and a propane stove. I dreamed of the forest every night and couldn't concentrate in class for thinking of everything that trip held in store.

My father had an enormous orange rucksack, the sort people used in the eighties, with a tubular structure at the bottom for stowing the tent. I'd take my school backpack, which was large enough to hold three changes of clothes, a Game Boy, and a compass—a Christmas present from some aunt that I didn't know how to use, but that seemed appropriate.

On the Friday, we got up at 6:00 a.m. and, while my father was having his coffee, the two of us made a heap of sandwiches and packed them in the Bimbo bread bag. Mom woke a little later and, still drowsy, prepared a couple of liters of flavored water with those sachets of powder that didn't taste of any real fruit, poured the liquid into two large bottles, and put them in the orange rucksack.

I don't know why we didn't take the car; it would have been simpler and more sensible. I guess my father wanted me to get a closer view of the country; to travel, just like anyone else, in a rusty bus with no suspension along the potholed state highways. It wasn't, at heart, just a simple adventure, but a journey with educational undertones; an opportunity to coexist with that Real World from which an excess of care—sporadically lamented by my father—distanced me.

My mother dropped us outside the downtown bus terminal. In contrast to the terminal in Casino de la Selva, which we used more frequently, the one in the center evoked journeys to undiscovered places, women with baskets containing live chickens, buses belonging to unknown lines, and a general smell of earth and food that had me in a state of nervous anticipation. Before going to buy the tickets, Dad suggested we have breakfast at a cart across the street. My dad has always liked eating street food, but Mom would see ameba and salmonella in every sauce, typhoid in every sandwich, and unhealthy fats in the filthy oil where the suadero sizzled. Taking advantage of being out of sight of his wife's reproving eye, Dad ordered two gordas de chicharrón with everything for himself and for me a tlacoyo de frijoles, which I wolfed down after removing the nopal.

The campsite was in El Chico, forty minutes from Pachuca. Or maybe it was the Los Azufres area of Michoacán with its thermal pools; I don't remember. The thing is that you couldn't get there directly from Cuernavaca, so we had to go to Mexico

City and wait thirty minutes before boarding a packed, beat-up local bus that would stop at several small towns en route. On the first leg of the journey, I slept almost the whole way, waking every so often to ask if we'd arrived yet and where that horrible smell was coming from ("no" and "from the restroom, I think the toilet's blocked" were my father's answers on each occasion). At Taxqueña terminal, Dad left me, half asleep, in charge of our belongings while he went to make some inquiry at a ticket office. When he returned, carrying our tickets and a can of Coca-Cola, the orange rucksack had disappeared.

We could have gone back to Cuernavaca and called off the trip, but I suspect my father wanted to avoid the humiliation of returning early and defeated, so we decided to continue on our way. Before boarding the second bus, Dad bought himself some clothes and two blankets at a stand in Taxqueña metro station and said we could rent a log cabin instead of camping, as we'd planned (our tent had disappeared along with the rucksack). I remember with a pain as piercing as the one now paralyzing my jaw just how guilty I felt about having ruined our trip: my only responsibility had been to keep an eye on our things, and I hadn't even been able to do that. I apologized over and over, but nothing he said could erase the disappointment I thought I discerned in my father's embittered smile, in the way he said, without believing it for an instant: Don't worry, it's not important.

I spent the whole time on that second bus obsessively reconstructing the crucial minutes when our things were stolen, but I never figured out just how it had happened.

We got off the bus at a bend in the road and walked along a path heading into the forest. The camp was on a hillside:

a stretch of open ground with a few cabins and the cottage where breakfast was served. The people with tents set up camp in scattered clearings in the forest, with enough space between them to build a fire. We, on the other hand, rented the only available cabin: little more than a wooden roof with a bare light bulb and walls of planks so poorly fitted that the wind entered as if it owned the place.

Luckily, we had the blankets from the stand in Taxqueña station, and they turned out to be as warm as any sleeping bag, although for me they tempered the excitement of the trip as, to be honest, what interested me was all the equipment, the professional side of camping. It would have been four or five in the afternoon, so we left our meager belongings on the cold concrete floor and went out to find coffee with cream (for my father) and hot chocolate (for me). I remember my surprise at seeing pine trees, accustomed as I was to the subtropical flora of Cuernavaca—flamboyants, coral trees, the peeling trunk of the guavas, and the parchment-like bark of the amates. A milky fog descended slowly over the camp and Dad explained—I didn't believe him—that we were in a cloud.

It rained that night and the cabin turned out to offer insufficient protection: water filtered through the gaps between the planks and the wind shook the whole structure. We wrapped ourselves as best we could in the blankets, but didn't sleep a wink all night, me from fright, my father trying his hardest to keep me dry.

The next morning, when Dad decided to cut short the trip and travel back to Cuernavaca, I didn't have the confidence to complain because I was still feeling the weight of guilt on my shoulders: the rucksack had been stolen from *me*.

Looking back, I think my father changed after that trip. He stopped trying to buddy up to me and became increasingly isolated within himself. He adopted a weird custom of sleeping in the garden, in a hammock strung from a high branch of the tulip tree. "I'm going to meditate outdoors," he'd say. He'd climb up to his hammock, five feet from the ground, toss a coarse green blanket that my mother hated over himself, and spend most of the night there, until the early morning chill forced him to give up on that eccentricity and return, resignedly, to the marriage bed and the insidious normality of his forty-something years. He spent two or three months like that, addicted to the outdoors, suspended in a hammock, in the dark garden, like an outlaw, ignoring my mother's reproofs: Come back inside, something will sting you out there.

I guess that sudden love of open skies was the only form of midlife crisis my dad—too shy to have lovers and too poor to buy a Harley-Davidson—allowed himself; his discrete way of distancing himself for a moment from the binary state of marriage in order to be unitary again, defending that—poetic or pre-Socratic—love of looking at the night sky.

I admired my father during his period of alfresco sleeping, but in a way that suggested my admiration was a shamefaced secret. I wasn't the sort of boy who boasted at school of his father's exploits, his spending power or dream job. I would, however, sometimes lose focus in class, stare out the window into the yard bathed in harsh sunlight, and think of its contrast to my father's moonbaths. I'd wonder, without actually putting it into words, what he thought about during those sleepless nights, rocked by the wind and surrounded by the scent of tulip tree blossom past its prime swooning beneath his hammock. For an adult to break the most sacred of conventions—sleeping in a bed when you're at home—in this way seemed to me an unsolvable mystery, an unknown that made me imagine adult life as a much more complex and nuanced territory than I'd initially supposed.

But the craze for outdoor sleeping passed. He returned to the marital bed and to the fold of norms and decorum. And with time, I too became an adult with more debts than illusions. A divorced adult, racked by pain, in whose memory glows—radioactive material—the recollection of a father who used to gaze at the stars. When I come to think of it, that memory might contain the seed of my interest in sensory deprivation tanks and John C. Lilly. Like my father, Lilly was a scientist who suffered a crisis of faith in the dogma on which science is based. He tried communicating with dolphins and floating in nothingness; for a number of nights, my father floated among the branches of the tulip tree.

Now my dad is an overweight, middle-aged man, anchored to the ground by common sense and a vague resentment. The hammock no longer hangs in the tulip tree and it hasn't rained for months in Cuernavaca. And I've been unable to make my own crisis into a pretext for changing my way of seeing the world.

Once again I wake during the night, in pain. I've lost count of the days, just as before I used to lose count of the hours. I don't know if I wake several times in one night or if a whole day goes by between each awakening. I don't know when I went to Conejo's, when I met Natalia, when I walked down the cobbled streets of Santa María Ahuacatitlán, or went to the Cine Morelos or the Amanalco Ravine to observe the effects of the drought (animal skeletons, hollow trunks). One Permutal pill later, I'm staring at the blotch on the ceiling, feeling light, my arms like colored ribbons someone has tied to my torso. For a moment, I can't make anything out, can't see any form there, any meaning. Noise and chaos. Then a new figure begins to take shape. A face in profile, as though it were in the process of turning, like in a blurred photo, into a sort of accidental Francis Bacon some painter and decorator had left there for me to see. There's something ominous about the melting face, that smudged portrait; but before I can decide just what it is, I fall asleep and serenely dream there's a wolf trapped in a classroom of the Instituto Arcadia.

The next morning, I leave home early and take a cab to Natalia's address in Santa María. I don't dare ring the bell in case Argoitia has returned from his trip, but I stand gazing at the green gate of the house from the grocery store on the corner while drinking a Coca-Cola. The storekeeper is chatting with a neighbor about the water shortage and I listen to her for a while, but then I get distracted by analyzing in obsessive detail the sensation of being me at that instant in time: what hurts, what throbs, what's bothersome or giving a little respite; what's creaky and what's asking to be moved.

I haven't had a shit in days, and there's an awful weight in my gut, some kind of lead in my intestines. I remember Conejo's pink dildo and shiver. Then I ask the storekeeper for another Coca-Cola and with the first sip realize it was a mistake; I feel something like disgust, not quite nausea, but a discomfort that's hard to pin down.

When I'm just about to leave, to return to my parents' house without seeing Natalia, the green gate opens and a car—a pickup really—comes out with the old guy at the wheel. Someone I can't quite make out closes the gate from inside.

I let five minutes pass before walking over and rapping timidly on the metal gate. Then I spot a chain hanging by the wall and pull it: a bell sounds somewhere far away inside, and a dog barks in a neighboring house, setting off a cascade of other barks. When the noise begins to die down, Natalia opens a sort of Judas window in the gate and her face is framed by the rapidly peeling green paint. Not her whole face, just her eyes and the bridge of her nose. Her mouth isn't visible and I can't imagine her expression on seeing me outside with a half-drunk Coke in my hand. Can I use your bathroom? I ask. I've got a stomachache. Gee, she says—imitating the dubbed voices of the gringo movies we used to watch on free-to-air in our childhood—you really know how to make a girl feel special. Then she closes the Judas window. For a moment I think she's going to leave me standing there, imagining the pink dildo in my rectum, with a sense of death in my gut, but then the metal door creaks and opens just enough for me to squeeze through. Come in quick, says Natalia, the neighbors spend the whole day gossiping.

The feel of the hot, flattened grass in the circle that had been occupied by an inflatable pool. The mild night fever after a day spent lying in the sun like vulture fodder, with sweat gathering in the fine hairs of the back of the neck, or burning in the corner of an eye, or descending slowly, thick as lava, down bronzed temples. The fullness of the body, its stubborn being-there, among other bodies, like a lump that does nothing besides cast a shadow; whose only function is to cast a shadow.

Another memory: that slight, subtle intoxication of adolescence, when the alcohol—whatever the quality—would make me feel freer, more in my skin than ever. Dancing without consideration for others, limbs following the instructions of some invisible being, as if guided by an intuition I've never since been able to channel. The sensation that even saliva has a taste loaded with meaning, that a smile or the blink of an eye are communicating every nuance of my desire to a person on the other side of the dance floor.

Or something close to sadness after fucking, both still lying there—a hand draped languidly over the bed base, the clothes heaped up in a corner, the fresh stains on the sheets—staring at the ceiling, but also at something beyond: a possible sky, an ephemeral paradise reached via weariness, with leg muscles slightly cramped, lips swollen from kissing and sucking and receiving bites; the light breeze on the skin of the thigh, on the skin of the chest rising and falling unevenly to the rhythm of still uneven breathing. I miss all those ways of being myself, of being fully, unquestionably inside myself without pain commandeering me, without the reminder that I'm dying, waning, falling headfirst into nothing, like a picnic left for the ants.

Natalia said I looked pale, ill. I made an awkward attempt to kiss her and she pushed me away gently. We sat on the couch in the study and she extracted the tequila flask from its hiding place in the bookshelves. (The same flask she took out the last time, a few—I'm not sure how many—days before, when I ran into her outside the Cine Morelos and came home with her, and it seemed like everything was going to go back to the way it was when we were kids, but then I lost my erection and any sense of where I was headed.)

Take a swig, she said, it'll do you good. For a moment I thought of the Permutal and ibuprofen I'd taken over the last days, of the multiple pills my liver had still to process. I only took a small sip, just wetting my lips, so as not to seem rude, but the tequila still burned on my tongue.

I told Natalia that I'd been walking around the city without recognizing it, that I'd gone to the lot where, as teenagers, we used to smoke poor-quality pot amid the bamboo, with the smell of sewage everywhere. Nowadays, I said, that plot is a shopping center with a ramshackle McDonald's and two budget pharmacies.

But Natalia wasn't listening; she was looking at me as though we spoke different languages. She interrupted to say she had to water her plants. I looked out the study window and saw the adobe wall with around ten epiphytes nailed to it like BDSM fairies. Natalia filled a mister with water and four drops of something or other, then went outside to water them, leaving me sitting there. I took advantage of the pause to place a Permutal tablet on a book (something about the art made by people with mental illnesses) and grind it with a stone ashtray that was on the coffee table. That blind spot between my shoulder and jaw was beginning to hurt again. I took out the same twenty-peso bill I'd used at Conejo's house—Benito Juárez's stern face seemed to be judging me from the polymer surface—took a deep snort, and when I raised my eyes, Natalia was staring at me in astonishment from outside the window. I had the sensation that she was moving in slow motion or maybe it was me slowing down as I melted into the dirty upholstery of the couch.

I don't know how or when I got here.

I'm back in my room, my childhood bedroom with the

same old bed, the blotch on the ceiling that has changed shape again: from my viewpoint, it looks like a wedding cake with two ducks emerging from it. (What kind of sinister celebration is encoded in that image? What sect practicing avian perversions conceived such an object?) I'm a little worried that the blotch is changing shape more often. My perceptual instability must be a symptom of a deeper imbalance. Looking at the ceiling now is like scrolling on the dark feed of the unconscious, like looking at a series of cards with Rórschach inkblots. I can't fix the image: the garden of my dreams has refused me entry.

I listen to the noise of the television filtering through the door—my deduction is that my parents are watching an action movie: there's that repeated sound of punches; a sound that doesn't exist in the real world, but that we've all agreed to associate with fistfights. The bedroom door is ajar but I can't be bothered to get up to close it. I haven't felt any pain in the last few hours, yet I know that's an illusion: the pain is still there, behind the analgesics, like a crouching Bengal tiger, camouflaged in the long grass.

The blotch on the ceiling has changed shape again. I plummet into senseless absurdity.

There used to be rainstorms that lasted several days, accompanied by frequent lightning and fallen trees. Real storms that transformed Cuernavaca's ravines into death traps for the neighborhoods clustered precariously on the slopes. The whole city would turn into a shambles, streets that overnight became rivers carrying rocks the size of dogs, vehicles with flooded engines, swamped tunnels, trees that suddenly looked taller, as though they alone separated the sky from the earth. For two or three months a year, rains would slash the city, the state, the whole country. News bulletins reported hurricanes with names like Ruby and Selene, which endangered ports and washed away whole stretches of coastline. At home, there were power outages; Dad would light candles and Mom would take out a deck of cards or tell horror stories with weird details, which were in fact laughable but stuck in my mind (a severed hand dancing tango, a curse that turned people into sleepwalkers). In the morning, branches would be strewn around the garden, as if the trees had lowered their guard and spread out to take a rest. At school, during recess, we kids would search for slugs in the planters and poke them with twigs—a muddy uniform and the threat of fresh rainstorms looming on the horizon.

It's been years since anything like that happened. The glorious downpours were replaced by drizzle that made only a slight impression between two dry periods. And then, this year, nothing. Wildfires broke out: at first they were attributed to cuts in the forestry commission budget, to potheads smoking in the hills, to tourists dropping glass bottles; the government attempted to put the blame on the opposition, who, in their version, set fires in the forest to generate instability and alarm. But the terror of those early days soon wore off and street vendors of face masks with ash filters began to offer new models without anything really changing. Children holding tight to their mothers' hands on the way to school looked up at the dull sky as if it had always been that way, and politicians entered the arena, creating new, juicier scandals for the media to vent their outrage on.

At the beginning of May, when wildfires devastated three communities minutes after they had been evacuated, it was mentioned only on page five of the newspapers, alongside a note about a robbery in a hardware store. In contrast, Don Profeta was in the headlines, urging his faithful followers to come together again in public squares to pray for salvation and the imminent ascent of their souls. The governor was at his side, handing him a bronze figurine in recognition of his work; he said that he himself was loyal to the state policy of laicism, but had to maintain a dialogue with the ecumenical community as a whole. And that was why he appeared each week in photographs with someone else. Catholic priests, faith healers, and pastors, all well-groomed, proudly displaying their crucifixes, silk ties, and gold teeth. Some had TV channels; others, former theaters converted into spectacular cult venues. But none were as famous or sinister as Don Profeta, who shouted poor paraphrases of the Apocalypse from his pulpit.

With the wildfires adorning the four points of the compass, certain members of the clergy also jumped on the bandwagon of apportioning blame; it was the sodomites, the feminists, Darwinism, or a combination of all those heresies plus the exasperation of God, who was amusing himself painting miniature hells in the most modest of plots on the outskirts of Cuernavaca just so we knew what was in store for us.

Some animal species, the ones that survived, escaped the flames by coming down into outlying areas of the city, particularly to the north. In Monte Casino, a notary shot a coyote from his window. In Santa María, very near where Natalia was living, a woman swore she'd spotted a stag. The same day, several people reported seeing a flock of more than twenty sparrow hawks flying at various points between Huitzilac and Temixco. But there were fires in other places too, so I guess all those creatures eventually found refuge, or were hunted, or fell exhausted on the roof of one of the two hundred shopping malls opened in the city in the past ten years.

All this happened over a period of months. I initially followed the events from Mexico City, while I was selling the last of my furniture and waiting for my severance pay to come through so I could afford the divorce lawyer's fee. Dad used to send me news via WhatsApp—photos with the top half cropped, inaccurate data, but also solid reports detailing an equally fucked-up reality—as though alerting me that it wasn't the best moment to return home.

Home. That single syllable contains so much and so little. A blotch I didn't remember in the paint; the sound of the TV heard from down the hallway; the bright, roomy kitchen with grease stains on the walls; the small garden with dried-out grass no one has watered since December; the bathroom mirror with rounded corners that reflects back to me features relaxed by the effects of Permutal but also tired or worn out: a face with a deep frown; a face with unsettling bags under the eyes and sallow skin, with a suddenly graying, receding hairline—the forehead progressively broader and emptier: a helipad where mild happiness and clear images no longer land, where there is nothing but shadow, fear, and a pained grimace.

Maybe everything would have been simpler if I hadn't convinced myself that I had talent.

I believed from an early age, without a shadow of doubt, that when I graduated from high school I'd move to Mexico City, start film school, and, when they viewed my first exercises, all the teachers would prostrate themselves before me, immediately recommending me for a study-abroad scholarship. By way of a thesis, I'd write and direct a movie short; a stunningly clear-cut piece of fiction about a teenage relationship, based on my time with Natalia, which would win all the Mexican prizes. And after that, a whole raft of opportunities would present themselves. I'd film in virgin rainforests and Asian cities with mile-high skyscrapers; I'd be known for my ability to delve beneath the banal. Thanks to my professional success, I'd have close relationships with women from an incredible variety of backgrounds who would all secretly be captivated by my charms, but it would never go any further: they would be sublime, platonic loves that, at most, would involve a kiss because, deep down, I'd still be in love with Natalia and dreaming of returning to Cuernavaca with a Palme d'Or and a Venice Golden Lion to swallow my pride and beg her to come back to me.

All those ambitions, chewed over during endless evenings watching the rain—in the days when it used to rain—set the scene for my disillusion. At eighteen, I was turned down for film school, and again at nineteen, and at twenty. I convinced my parents to fund a diploma at a private school that had a reputation for "putting you in touch with industry people," which meant being used as unpaid labor in the production of infomercials. Years later, I found a job in the organization of a film festival and for a time the contact with directors and actresses allowed me to reassume my air of misunderstood creative artist. But cinema is such a collective activity that the myth of the solitary genius very soon falls flat: by my thirtieth birthday, all I wanted was to save enough money to be able to afford a place to live that didn't involve sharing with four other bastards just as depressed and empty as myself, even if it was in a neighborhood with no cafés or restaurants.

I met Lucía at an event during the film festival; an open-bar cocktail party in the courtyard of a private university, with smoked salmon canapés, dubious mezcal, and nineties music that everyone danced to ironically. Lucía poked fun at the general ambience, the festival, and the world of cinema before asking me what I did for a living. When I shamefacedly explained, she gave a hoot that made me think she was drunk.

Half an hour later we snuck off to a secluded area of the venue and kissed in a corridor smelling of cat piss.

Lucía persuaded me to leave the party and accompany her and her friends to another in an apartment in Colonia Narvarte. In the cab on our way there, her friends covertly grilled me as though I was a pretender for her hand. And, truth be told, there was something promising and harmonious about that fortuitous encounter; an outburst of desire and coquetry that, in my imagination, might lead to a stable relationship.

By the time we got to her place—at seven in the morning—we were so tired and drunk that we didn't even go through the pantomime of fucking: we flopped onto the bed in what we were wearing, with an unbearably needy cat purring loud as a truck a few centimeters from the pillow.

I make this summary after midnight, napping for short periods and then continuing. I wake four or five times during the night, bathed in sweat, too hot under the blankets. On each occasion, I retain only the final images of a dream, isolated scenes, without the least hint of a plot or explanation: a play that had to be watched from a hot-air balloon, a female cab driver who takes the long way around, a yellowing garden full of tlacuaches—their elusive ratlike tails electrifying the landscape.

The last time I wake it's still dark, although dawn isn't far off: it's a sneaking suspicion beyond the branches of the tulip tree, an indistinct murmur beginning to take form. I decide not to sleep any longer and walk noiselessly to the kitchen, where I eat half a small papaya, sitting in the place usually occupied by my mother. My gut is making strange noises, like a building about to collapse. The constipation has morphed from an annoyance to a metaphor: a complete inability to process anything, the grip of a dog's jaws on another dog's neck. Maybe the fruit will help.

The sun begins to come up and the first birds appear, warbling frantically, as though welcoming the last morning of planet Earth. My back feels stiff and there's a promise of pain to come in the upper vertebrae of my neck, just about where the spinal column connects to the cranium. I stand up, rotate my head slowly in wide circles then move it from side to side, like I'm saying no to life.

Back in my bedroom, I consider the possibility of jacking off, but to be honest, my libido has been at a very low ebb for ages.

It's strange. Like most teenagers, I was obsessed with sex, which meant I was incapable of leaving my dick alone for more than six hours, and for a long time the same was true in my adult life, with the associated negative effects on my relationships, my emotional stability, my reputation, and my work. These days, all I feel is a stone in my gut and the need to take Permutal in order to tolerate my body. My body is the enemy; it doesn't trust itself, eyes itself suspiciously as though awaiting the traitorous shot that will end it all. My body is the beast and the zookeeper, and the children whose mouths form an *oh* of surprise when they see the gorilla hurl its shit around, and the man at the hot-dog cart, and the clouds too: my body is the dull, dark clouds through which pass crazed, squawking grackles, while down below a man shouts: Get your antifungal nail cream here.

Lack of sleep. That must be the problem.

•

I decide I need to do something to ward off the possibility of becoming addicted, which is no joke. I've been addicted to a number of substances in the past and I don't want to go through that again. Today I'll try not to take Permutal and go back to ibuprofen and acupuncture. I might be able to find a Chinese doctor here in Cuernavaca who will apply a plaster smelling of egg that will miraculously cure me in an instant. Or better still, the psychiatrist who treated Helena Paz Garro will offer me the same prescription she gave Helenita when she was living in isolation with her mother, Elena, near the ruins of Teopanzolco; some nonaddictive pill with a pearly coating that will lighten me up. But in the meantime . . .

At 7:15 in the morning, before Mom and Dad wake, I leave the house quietly and take a cab downtown, carrying an old backpack rescued from the closet, containing nothing more than ten ibuprofen, a bottle of water, and a detective novel.

Downtown, everything is still shut; there are women sweeping the dust and ash from their corresponding stretch of sidewalk and then going back indoors, satisfied to have set a piece of the world in order. A street cleaner whistles a cumbia, watched by the indolent eyes of a dog that lazily moves aside to allow him to pass. Farther off, someone raises the metal gate of a shoe store and, without warning, I feel a new stab of pain around my collarbone.

I sit on the steps in Plazuela del Zacate. A drunk passes by, loudly singing a song about lost love, and behind me, a cabdriver stops to clean his windshield, which is coated in the sort of smutty dust that's been covering everything for the last six days. A man selling pan dulce also passes on a bicycle and I buy an instant coffee from him and gulp it down with a look of disgust. The whistling street sweeper swerves to avoid a flock of office workers hurrying to get to their desks on time. When I look up, the almost stationary clouds form the same changeable shapes as the blotch on the ceiling above my bed. I lean against a wall and the cold stone feels comforting. I drowse there for a while, with the generous permission of my body.

At ten o'clock I decide to walk around the downtown area, following the same route of seven or eight streets I used to take when I was a teenager and looking for Conejo or Natalia. It was a sort of courtship ritual. The three of us would set out on random paths through that quadrant and, when we happened to meet, we'd take a few more turns through the streets before going our separate ways again. Sometimes it was just Natalia and me, at others Conejo found her first and they walked together. Whenever we were a threesome, one of us would feel excluded and decide to split off. We never spoke during those strange holding patterns that united and separated our routes. Our ritual was a fact of life, as real as the walls or the cars around us. The world presented itself to us as finished, a place we couldn't modify very much.

While remembering all that, I pass the Museo Brady. Its

collection of masks, which I glimpse from the street, reminds me of my own grimaces of pain. I tell myself that I'm the jaguar-man when I have a stabbing pain in my shoulder; the eagle-warrior when I wake in the middle of the night with my jaw stinging; I'm that devil with the twisted smile after snorting Permutal. And I momentarily repent not having stayed home until I'd taken the last of the pills, happily sedated in the shade of the tulip tree.

I continue walking through the streets—only partially recognizing them—as though I were an earlier version of myself who, on every corner, relived a three-way relationship I then completely forgot.

When I notice that the Jardín Borda is open, I decide to go in and rest for a while by one of the fountains. And there, on the billboard beside the ticket office where performances are listed—while I feel the sun on the back of my neck, a bead of sweat trickling down my rib cage, a stab of pain in my jaw—a familiar face smiles out at me among the announcements posted by the Ministry of Culture: *The Great Noise*. A dance choreographed by Natalia Ahumada. Thursday, June 21, 7 p.m. Lakeside Stage. The day after tomorrow. I'll take a ticket for the dance too, I tell the assistant, who hasn't yet looked at me: she's staring through me at some vague spot in space, at something behind my head, perhaps my ghost. I put the ticket in one of the pockets of my backpack and continue into the garden. There's a spindly night-blooming jasmine growing by the veranda of the main house.

The garden is unrecognizable: the plants withering, some of them uprooted from the planters; the pond that—in exaggeration—is known as the lake has been drained and all that can be seen there now are the slimy bed and a few islands of accumulated trash: plastic bags, a worn-out shoe, generalized filth. Even the trees seem to have admitted defeat: a stunted Mexican cypress leans against a section of wall that was never repaired after the earthquake two years ago. A gardener is collecting dead plants and putting them in a large garbage bag; he has a gravedigger air, as though, during the drought, his job has become sinister and marginalized, blighted. I stop to pass the time of day with him. He tells me they have had no water for three weeks; the city council has asked them to use the water in the pond for the plants, but now the pond is empty and there's little else to be done. He says all this almost robotically, in a resigned tone, devoid of sentimentality. Then he confirms my suspicion that the cypress had been in danger of falling since the earthquake, but with the earth now so dry, it had finally perished.

I nod my head in farewell, walk on to a fountain—it isn't running—and sit down. From here I can see the structure of the garden's museum, which has an exhibition of lousy drawings by amateur artists on the theme of Maximilian of Hapsburg (or Mexico). It must be in one of the museum's rooms or the small auditorium where Natalia holds her rehearsals, putting the final touches to *The Great Noise*. It will be a depressing spectacle, I think, with the dancers wearing face masks to protect themselves from the ash floating in the air, performed behind a pond full of flies, Coca-Cola bottles, and dead algae. But then it occurs to me that's exactly the kind of setting Natalia would want: anything that throws light on the unbearable pretension and tedious poverty of the municipal middle class to which we belong.

From the fountain, I can just make out an aluminum sign nailed up in one of the arid gardens next to a swooning flamboyant tree. "This garden belongs to you. If you like it, don't let your children destroy it." I read it several times, with the sensation of having seen those words somewhere else. Perhaps there was a similar sign in Chapultepec, where I used to go every morning for years to run two or three kilometers, when I was happily resident in Mexico City—happily married, with no pain, no Permutal, and a steady job: a combination that now, months later, seems highly unlikely, imaginary, something nobody is capable of having all at once. And then, suddenly, I remember; the sign in my dream: "This garden belongs to us all, but only those with a clear-cut vision can enter."

The pain has made me way too conscious of my own body. I observe myself as though under a microscope, with the magnifying lens of the conscience. Sitting here, amid the dead plants and crumbling walls of the Jardín Borda, my eyes closed, I run a check on my whole body in search of some symptom, some sign, a vanquished region. An enemy.

In my right elbow, I detect a slight inflammation that might worsen at any moment. At the back of my neck, the tension of vertebrae digging into the brain continues. And in my gut, the leaden weight of constipation that modifies the force the Earth exercises on me. My leg is trembling.

I swallow an ibuprofen without water, just in case, and regret not having brought the Permutal. If I were able to take a couple of pills right now, in fifteen minutes life would be much simpler. The gardener would come across me semi-comatose among the dry leaves of the Jardín Borda with an infantile grin on my face.

The thought of that placidity makes me anxious and I begin walking around the garden without making any decision. I remember a Japanese restaurant somewhere nearby that I used to visit regularly as a teenager; it had a small private room, almost always free, where you sat on the floor to eat at a low table. I usually just ordered lemonade because I didn't have money for sushi. The room was littered with cushions and the waiters would let me nap there while I waited for Natalia to come find me or Conejo to invite me to his house, where he and I sometimes made out with a sort of desperation or urgency, but never going further than kissing, as if exploring that form of nonverbal communication was enough for us.

I decide to go to the Japanese restaurant—if it still exists—but as I'm leaving the garden, I pass an open door to one of the salons and, out of the corner of my eye, notice a strange movement. Hidden by the door frame, I peep inside. Bodies abruptly falling onto floorboards, sudden leaps, sonorous exhalations, and contortions on the ground. And moving among the bodies, again—forever—Natalia.

I wake during the night in a sweat, feeling I can't breathe. The pain has now moved to my left elbow, like an off-center heart. I'm probably mutating, I think. I'll probably wake up converted into some disgusting insect stuck on the blotch on the ceiling I've been keeping such a careful watch over for almost a whole lifetime. Or, more likely, I may have some form of cancer, or an undiagnosed autoimmune condition: my body attacking itself. Anticipating the onslaught of a nonexistent enemy, my white blood cells fabricate opponents in the tissues of my joints and attack them without mercy. It's not beyond the realm of possibility. I recognize that procedure in many things I do: I invent adversaries and even whole plots to do away with me, but I then discover they are—invariably—projections of self-inflicted contempt. And just the same is happening inside me, in the viscous darkness of the blood—unknown territory; my personal verdant jungle; a wild country where everything is decided, despite the fact that it pretends just the opposite.

I wake during the night in pain. No animal is making a sound. The air in the room seems stale, heavier than usual. The heat makes me think the wildfires have finally reached the city. Shopping malls in flames. Beer warehouses, botaneras, seafood restaurants, stands selling tacos acorazados, pretentious restaurants with European names—the Vivaldi, the Café Vienés—the four mezcal bars that have opened in the last two years . . . All lit from within by the forked tongues of fire licking the walls until the paint blisters. Everything except this house: this besieged bastion, stronghold, bunker, protected by the air of my own childhood—the blotch on the ceiling, the very same bed. My parents will be eating papaya when the wildfire knocks at the door: "Don't answer it, my dear. Let's finish breakfast." And they will go on as normal, while the world gives way like a burned-out roof beam and the last surviving insects—those roaring sparks, those ascending flames, aspiring to be bright stars—crackle and buzz over the ashes of a planet with beautiful rubble and ruins.

One pill taken orally, a half snorted. Just to see if the elbow sorts itself out—it looks red, swollen, and fragile.

Yesterday, after her rehearsal, Natalia and I walked for a while downtown, like when we were kids. Without saying a word, we strolled along the same streets and both knew that, at heart, we were looking out for Conejo, who might appear at any moment, smiling cheerfully after stealing a piece of animal-print cloth from the fabric store: What's up, guys? How about a beer?

One of David Alfaro Siqueiros's models used to live in this house, Natalia said unexpectedly as we passed a front door like any other. Doña María Asúnsolo, she added; who was in fact Dolores del Río's cousin. She lived here with her iguanas until 1999, sunbathing nude in the garden of the house and scandalizing the neighbors, who could see her from their windows: a bronzed hide on a lounger, a straw hat, a straight tequila on a table at her side. How do you know that? I asked with a smile. Conejo told me, he had it from his father; as you're well aware, Señor Bertini knows every miserable corner of the city and has a story for all of them. And then, in a mocking tone, as if winding me up, she added: Those of us who have stayed here know a great many things. She takes pleasure in needling me for going to the capital. For going there and then coming back. I guess that circle is a little risible: there's something epic or mysterious about the ones who leave never to return, whereas those of us who do come back—the same people, only worse—inspire nothing but laughter.

Even so, Natalia knows there's also something sad and a little comical about having stayed. Always here, in Cuernavaca, like you're waiting for an opportunity that never appears.

She went on: Learning those ridiculous details is the only means we have of avoiding suicide; you have to unearth the stories this small town hides behind its walls. If we made do with what we can see, we wouldn't survive the week.

After that, we passed the CMA and I asked Natalia if she remembered the time we hid there to fuck in the basement. That building was a hospital in the nineteenth century, and what is now the basement used to be the morgue. When she went there for her dance classes and I went to photography, people used to tell horror stories about that part of the building: women appearing with their dresses bathed in blood, the sound of dogs barking behind walls . . . On that particular occasion, Natalia and I jerked each other off among piles of junk, canvases, easels, and folding chairs. But she said she didn't remember, and that made me doubt if the episode really had happened as I recalled it. Most likely it was a memory I invented years later; a recurring fantasy of a glorious past in a provincial city, while my bosses were bullying me or my wife was asking me to try harder to talk about my feelings. An invented episode, but nonetheless important—a yardstick, shall we say, or geological evidence of a private Pangea: that long-past time when the psyche was one, not a bunch of pieces scattered on the rug, like a jigsaw puzzle after an attack by a cat.

I suggested to Natalia that we could sleep together, get a room in the hotel in *Under the Volcano* or walk to the forest near where she lived and camp out there, as we used to when we were kids. There are wildfires all over the place, Erre, she said. And don't take it personally, but I have no intention of dying in your arms, and having us found the next day covered in ash, like a cheap imitation of the lovers of Pompeii. I accompanied her until she hailed a passing cab and then continued walking alone for quite a time in the direction of Conejo's.

Señor Bertini told me that Conejo wasn't home, but he invited me in for a drink. I've only got rum, he apologized, and there should be a bottle of cane liquor somewhere, but that makes you blind, he added with a sinister laugh. Señor Bertini's eyes sometimes open a little wider than usual and you can see that dense fog clouding the black of his iris.

He served me a cuba libre (I hope you don't mind, he said, but I added the ice with my own hands) and sat at the dinner table with an air of debauchery, as though we'd arranged to meet in some seriously seedy botanera. I guessed he'd already had a few.

So, tell me, he began, why did you come back to Cuernavaca? Conejo said you're divorced. Is that right? I glanced at him and took a swig of my drink, which was too strong. Yes. Can you believe it? Seven years of marriage, and then I'm out on my ass. Señor Bertini laughed again, with that coarse laugh, just like his son's. Ay, Erre, they gave it to you good, but look on the bright side: you're still young and more or less in one piece; I was left wrinkled, blind, and alone. Not alone, I replied, you have Conejo. Señor Bertini raised his glass to his lips and, just before taking a sip, muttered: All the worse, my boy. All the worse.

The days fly past but months stretch out forever. When I had a job, a routine, and a savings account it was just the opposite: days as slow as dripping honey and years that lasted less time than the domestic arguments. That was before all this.

Dad is concerned about my physical health, though it's his own he should be worried about. He says I'm thinner than usual, that I'm all skin and bones and, with my hair mussed up, I look like a sucked mango. He opens a beer and stands looking at the dry grass in his small garden. There's been no rain for ages and the little water left in the tank is for essentials only. Dad puts a hand under his shirt to pat his belly and asks me to go to the market to buy the things on the list they keep by the phone: Your mom can't do everything, he adds with a frown—as a child, his frowns inspired me with almost mythic terror. An expression that means, "You're standing on a cliff edge and I'm just longing to give you a push." Every man I know has a variant on that facial expression: nostrils suddenly flared, carotid artery visible in the neck, the corners of the mouth pursed in a slightly menacing smile. Every man except Conejo.

We enjoyed making out when we were young. At first, we didn't dare unless alcohol or drugs were involved, or in situations that in some way justified the display of affection: a rave in Temixco, a night on the tiles in Mexico City, the day his dad didn't recognize him in the street and we drank a two-liter bottle of pulque sitting on a rock in the ravine. Then we began to do it in a quieter way, on his bedroom floor, on nights when we were talking about what we wanted to do when we were fully fledged adults.

After a session of touching and exchanging saliva, I'd always have the bad taste to tell him that I wasn't interested in men. Conejo would look away, hurt, and lock himself in the bathroom for a while. When he came out, he'd be more composed, distant, ready to go along with the ridiculous fiction that we weren't in love. Neither of us ever said anything about it to Natalia, or at least he swore he hadn't.

When Natalia and I split up, the sexual tension I experienced with Conejo also eased a little. For some strange reason that neither of us understood, our love was linked to the catalytic presence of Natalia, who somehow made us gentler, more sensitive. When she distanced herself from us, she took with her—in my case, permanently—that state of grace that used to run through my body on libidinous summer evenings, when it was raining outdoors and inside, in whoever's room, it was all skin, curiosity, and tongues.

Later, in Mexico City, I had sex with several women and the occasional man but never again experienced that total dissolution of the dermal frontier I'd had with Natalia and Conejo at the age of seventeen. I sometimes think that the pain, or at least its seed, began then, when I detached myself from the three-way union that made us all luminous.

But the true germ of that pain and its rapid development could in fact be charted from the register of symptoms I began to keep a few months ago. (It's a pity that log isn't more accurate: some nights I note where the pain has been during the day, but others I forget to do it.)

It began as a sort of presentiment: the sudden awareness that some part of my body existed, as though it had previously been hidden from me. I attributed it to the stress of those days: the divorce, unemployment, the thought that I might have to return to Cuernavaca and get my life back on track from my parents' house. Then that presentiment became more intrusive. Like a sugar cube in contact with black coffee, the pain gained increasingly more ground at a constant rate. The larger joints were affected. At night the world dissolved and the solipsism of pain would have me howling until first light.

Now, in contrast, it's a sort of dance: a daimon that alights with variable intensity on a different part of my body every few hours, causing me to contract certain muscles, grimace, touch my arm, and contort my body in the middle of the street, under a flamboyant tree, as I walk through downtown Cuernavaca.

The simple act of advancing, of putting one foot in front of the other, becomes a battle for territory, the attempt to retake the fortified tower ceded to the enemy. Every order from the brain is a vanguard, a campaign to reclaim my natural rights over that leg, that elbow, that finger joint. I sometimes win the battle: the pain retreats for a few moments and I once again feel in charge. Then comes the counterattack. After a step, the pulsing tremor: the ankle surrenders to its own doubts and I limp slightly.

A voice unexpectedly interrupts my ruminations on possessive pain: Erre, what the fuck! Is that really you? Followed by a hug, the scent of cardamom, and a lock of curly black hair brushing my face. The woman takes a step back and says: What are you doing here? I haven't seen you for centuries. It seems an effort for her to smile: you can see she's gotten out of the habit and only recently decided to force herself back into it, but there's a profound sadness behind her teeth.

Don't you remember me? I'm Claudia, she says on noticing my blank expression. I look at her again, more carefully. A memory begins to stir, but doesn't quite take shape. Claudia, of course. How are you? I'm making a poor show of recognizing her and feel a stab of pain in my jaw, like a punishment for lying. Her sad, forced laughter says she knows I don't remember her.

But Claudia is very good-looking, I think; I really should remember a face like that. She has a few premature crow's feet, but they highlight her eyes, the pupils dilating and contracting with the changes of light when she passes under a tree.

We walk to a mezcal bar because she says she doesn't want to be outdoors for long: she's had a bad cough for days because of the wildfires. I use generic questions to try to discover where I know her from: How's life? Have you been in Cuernavaca all these years? She says no, she's lived in Mexico City and Barcelona; she had a short-lived career as an actor and is now a life coach. But I figure she doesn't walk the talk. Apparently, she came back to Cuernavaca because her dad lent her an apartment behind his house (pretty much the same as me, I think). She wants to open a pizzeria, or go to Oaxaca, or maybe study something new, like psychology or acupuncture, she says, as though they were the same professions. Her way of hesitating and changing the subject suddenly seems familiar. The memory struggles to rise to the surface, but something is dragging it back down to the bottom of the lake, eventually leaving only the bubbles of the drowned recollection. Just when I've given it up for dead comes a gulp of air, a kicking out in the calm waters of oblivion. Claudia aged fifteen, sitting in the cafeteria of the Instituto Arcadia, holding a pocket mirror to put on lipstick. That's it: we were in high school together.

The mezcal bar is a narrow cavern with three tables, a basic counter, and a menu of four items. Claudia orders for us both and the waiter returns with two shot glasses and segments of orange. You were my platonic love in high school, she says, and lifts her glass with a look of complicity I attempt to return, but I spill a little of the mezcal and instead of saying *salud*, what comes out is *sorry*. We drink in silence for a time, smiling but awkward. It was most probably a bad idea to agree to go to a bar with a person who has just emerged from my distant past. Any form of nostalgia immediately fizzles out, leaving a sort of hangover.

Fortunately, Claudia breaks the silence. She tells me that Natalia and I were the most popular of the nonpopular couples at school. I find that category both amusing and accurate and for a moment forget that my body is possessed, forget the pain lacerating me. She tells me she was friends with us both, and also with Conejo, and that the four of us sometimes went to exhibitions together and we used to dance and declaim poetry in public spaces, to the bewilderment of passersby. That's news to me, but this time I'm grateful for the memory lapse because I feel slightly ashamed of the things she's telling me.

Like Natalia, she started to study dance, she explained, but then she changed to drama and "kind of" made a living from that: she appeared in a few commercials and in a foreign movie filmed in Chachalacas, in which she had just one line, "We are luminous creatures." We laugh, and this time I have the sense that there's a sweet harmony forming between us, a brief moment of complicity.

She asks about my job and I tell her I'm unemployed. She says she remembers my parents' house, the exact address, the tulip tree in the garden, my room, the bed with yellow tubes. For a moment I consider asking her if she remembers the blotch on the ceiling over that bed, but I resist the temptation. How can this woman possibly know so much about my life when I've almost totally erased any memory of her? (I still have only that image in the cafeteria.) Could it be due to my high levels of drug consumption over various years? Due to the fact that I gave up on Cuernavaca the way you kick a habit, that I extracted myself from the city like an appendectomy?

Perhaps my physical pain has a neurological correlate: a silent devastation that is stealing whole parts of my life without my knowledge.

When we leave the bar, the sky is dark, although not completely. The deep blue of late afternoon has been replaced by the dull brown produced by the fires. Just like the day of the evangelical mass, the grackles are making a racket in the tops of the rubber trees. I'm tipsy but, miraculously, pain-free. I grab Claudia's hand, as if we were lovers, and she laughs again. For a moment I toy with the idea of going with her, of sleeping with the cardamom scent of her hair or fucking the whole night long. But I don't really want to have sex, and neither does she. At times, it's easy to confuse any form of sadness or anxiety with desire; I've talked about this with friends and it's happened to us all, particularly the men: we translate more complex feelings into the simplistic language of lust and hunger. I need a body, not sex: need to regain control over my extremities and oust the sprite that's shattering me internally.

Claudia stops by a neon beer sign and I understand that, true to her profession, she's chosen the best lighting for saying goodbye: the dimples in her cheeks when she smiles make me wish I were someone else, someone more lighthearted, less fucked up, or at the very least more willing to change. But the truce has come to an end: I'll return to wandering the downtown streets alone until I make the decision to head back to my parents' house. We hug and I say I hope we'll meet again.

On my own now, in solitude, I discover that the mezcal has produced a weird short circuit with the painkillers. I feel as though the insides of my shoes were suddenly softer, lined with velvet. That sensation begins to ascend from my feet to other parts of my body. A sense of lassitude, a pliable drowsiness, accompanied by the auditory hallucination of a major chord played on a church organ. In a moment of clarity (a clarity that's aware of the threat of the unconscious, that rages against "the dying of the light"), I decide I can't go back to my parents' house, not on foot, nor in a cab. It would be dangerous, I think: I could lose consciousness at any moment. Just at that instant I pass a seedy hotel in one of the streets running at right angles to Avenida Morelos in the direction of the Mercado Santos Degollado and go in. I ask for a room and the desk clerk, who has a squint and a lovely mole on her forehead, offers the choice of one with a fan or another with en suite. I ask if there's a room with both and, as she doesn't respond, assume that's too much to hope for, so I say I'll take the en suite. She smiles as she hands me the key (glued to a piece of wood with the name of the hotel in pyrogravure) and I gaze at her mole like someone looking through a telescope, and getting his first glimpse of an unnamed galaxy.

Five minutes later, still fully dressed except for my tennis shoes, I'm dribbling onto a pistachio-green throw with burn marks.

I wake in the night, but this time there's no blotch—that trigger of my imagination—on the ceiling. In its place is the immaculate ceiling of the hotel room and, where it meets the wall, a cobweb. The light of a streetlamp filters through the threadbare curtains and casts a few shadows, which I momentarily manage to substitute for the blotch. But that scene rapidly changes with the irruption of dawn and, after a while, the morning light fills the room, erasing any fantasy.

I make a quick internal check of my body and conclude that, for the moment, there's no sign of pain, although I am incredibly hungry: I feel like my intestines have started to consume themselves, dark ouroboros of my belly. The sight of the green blanket brings a moment of remorse: I really should have returned to my parents' house. But it's too late for that now.

I try to switch on my phone and discover that the battery is dead. As I'm leaving the hotel, I ask where I can get breakfast and the desk clerk with the mole on her forehead says there's a café on the corner, but she's not sure if there will be anybody there because almost all the other businesses have closed. Then she tells me that if I'm not planning to come back, I need to settle up. Given the alcohol and my general state of confusion, I can't really remember if I paid when I registered so I hand over the bills without argument and silently say goodbye to her lovely mole.

The café is as dirty and suspect as the seedy hotel, but I decide to go in anyway because it's the only place open within sight: the streets have that lethargic Sunday air.

I order huevos a la mexicana and, while I'm shoveling them down, browse a tabloid newspaper that has been left on the next table. As I read the first headline on the page where the paper has been left open ("They had to dance with the ugliest one!") I realize for the first time that it's June 22, not 21.

I've somehow lost a day and so have missed Natalia's performance, which I'd bought a ticket for. My parents must be thinking I've either been kidnapped or spent two days drunk at Conejo's. He, in turn, must be thinking I've been taken away on a UFO, or that I was too frightened to attend Natalia's event because that idiot Argoitia would be there.

I ask the waiter if he has a phone charger, but he quickly says no and disappears through a door. The newspaper article says two people were hit by a vehicle and killed while dancing in the middle of the street. I assume this is poetic license on the part of the journalists, that the people weren't dancing, but having an argument or brawling: it's common for that kind of low-life newspaper to use what you might call lyrical language.

I pay for my breakfast at the counter and leave the café, thinking of visiting Natalia in Santa María Ahuacatitlán to ask her forgiveness for missing the performance. I'll deal with my parents' worries later (if they are indeed worried: I'm probably just suffering a regression to adolescence).

While I'm waiting for a cab to pass, I attempt to reconstruct what happened. Did I sleep through a whole day in a sleazy hotel? And did I actually meet a past acquaintance called Claudia or was it just an invention of my disordered psyche? I decide the most plausible explanation is that the mix of mezcal and painkillers put me out of action, that I should have read the warning label before pouring three straight shots down my gullet. Never trust mezcal. Whatever the case, I can wave goodbye to the illusion of having a healthy friendship with Natalia: she'll never forgive me for not turning up.

The cabbie drives like he's at the end of his tether: he takes a route I don't recognize, that includes all the underpasses and bridges constructed over recent years. At the same manic speed of his driving, he talks about the news of the road deaths; according to him, the people weren't dancing; they were having convulsions in the street. The government is covering something up, he says with an air of knowing everything there is to know about what goes on behind the scenes in politics. This has to do with the fires and the contaminated water. People get sick and go crazy. Just look at those evangelists, talking such garbage: saying some of them are going to disappear in a flash and who knows what the fuck else. When someone disappears around here, it's because they've talked too much, and they don't end up in heaven but in one of those mass graves in Temixco.

While I generally agree with what he says, I don't give him much encouragement in case it might fuel his ardor. My head is in no state to be thinking of traffic accidents and evangelists. Instead, I try to come up with an excuse to offer Natalia. I'd texted her to say I'd see her at the performance and wasn't worried about Argoitia being there. She'd texted back: Bet you won't come, as if daring me, and now fate and pharmaceuticals have proved her right.

Pain returns from its vacation. This time it's in my hip, where the head of the femur slots into the socket. Sitting in the back of the cab, my knees bent, it isn't too painful, but I foresee difficulties in walking up the steep streets of Santa María (cabdrivers rarely want to go that far up the hill: they say the cobbles mess up their suspension, or ask for more money and then complain the whole way).

But this cab comes to a halt much sooner than I'd expected, when we'd scarcely arrived in Santa María. There appears to have been an accident or a robbery ahead of us: a Ruta 3 bus has stopped halfway up the hillside and behind it is a long tailback of vehicles with despairing drivers and a general sense of chaos. The cabdriver takes my fare and, after performing a complex, illegal maneuver, proceeds back down the same street.

Every step I take sparks the pain in my hip, as if something inside there is about to dislocate. But there's no alternative: I want to reach Natalia's. I have a keen sense of guilt about missing her event, about sleeping through a whole day on the green blanket of a sleazy hotel. I feel that only Natalia can offer me the forgiveness that I'm really begging of the world: forgiveness for breathing this filthy air that could be more use to others and occupying this space that I could just as well cede to the ants. And after Natalia's house, I think, I'll walk back down—or go on my knees, like someone on a personal, arbitrary pilgrimage—to Conejo's, and I'll ask his forgiveness, too, for standing him up, and for having spent years saying there was nothing between us, pretending to be mature, cool, and straight, when the only thing I really want, have always wanted, is to jump over the fence of a vacant lot to make out with him among the junk like the adolescents we were.

Only love can quench the fires.

Grimacing with pain, I walk as far as the chaotic scene: a group of fifteen or twenty people are watching a smaller group, who are writhing on the ground, leaping and skipping on the cobbles. The first idea that comes into my head on seeing them is that it looks like what I glimpsed at Natalia's rehearsal, but wilder. I also think that what they are doing must really hurt, but the dancers don't seem to react to any of the impacts and just continue moving as though they were made of rubber (although in fact at least two of them have bruises and visible wounds; one is bleeding). I consider asking someone what the hell is going on, but the shocked faces of the bystanders lead me to suspect that nobody really knows, so I skirt the group and continue on, bearing my own body with difficulty.

A few blocks up the hill, just before reaching my destination, I feel my stomach contracting and I double over, but nothing comes out. Bent over, looking down, I spot a dead gecko between the stones—the mere skeleton of a gecko neatly cleaned by ants. A fresh bout of retching contracts my stomach, and the spasm causes something in my hip to make a thunderous noise and then settle back into place, with the resulting disappearance of the pain. But I don't have a chance to enjoy the sense of relief before a third bout of retching leaves me on my knees. And then a fourth and a fifth bring me to my feet and carry me, stumbling and trembling, along the street, past the gate of Natalia's house, to the edge of the forest known as El Tepeite.

Bioluminescent Beach

My dad is always saying that he's ready to die, that he's more than achieved all his goals, even though he hasn't brought about a revolution, though my mother's left him and he's lived with blindness for many years. He claims that his only regret is not having grandchildren. But you can't regret that, I tell him, because it's my decision, not yours, but he thinks that's a technicality and brushes it aside with a wave of the hand and a melancholy half smile. It's not important, he says; other than that, I've had a splendid life.

That kind of suicidal vitality, coming from someone who, despite being pretty healthy, proclaims himself ready to go while simultaneously gloating over his passage through the world, is one of the many traits of my father's personality that I've never completely figured out. From an objective viewpoint, his life seems rather sad: a not particularly brilliant career as a historian of the conquest and the early colonial period in Morelos State, a marriage that ended in unfaithfulness, and a son—me—who's never shown the faintest sign of leaving home and whose only ambitions are to earn enough to buy marijuana, feed the local stray cats, and order pizza on Tuesdays to take advantage of the 2-for-1 offer.

But I both admire and am bewildered by my father's unjustified, self-destructive happiness; it's an optical illusion whose hidden mechanism makes me want to believe, if only for an instant, in magic.

There's a kind of justice in the fact that he has, over the years, succeeded in inspiring that form of incredulous admiration in me. For a long time he seemed the dullest of men, and that resigned joy of his, which today feels worthy of a mystic or a dervish, up until not so long ago was like a sign of tacky conformity that I wanted no part of.

Among my friends' parents, Dad was always the oldest, and when we were small, other kids used to tease me that he looked more like a grandfather. Our parents' lives before our birth exist in a kind of mythic time preceding the separation of land and water, like the lives of those original pre-Hispanic gods—often associated with amphibians—on whose death other deities were born to reign over worldly things.

In Dad's case, the story of that long, convoluted prehistory claims that he was active in a small Maoist-inspired student group, doomed to failure, that hoped to bring about a revolution in three or four municipalities of Morelos during the seventies. They were a bunch of sixteen- and seventeen-year-olds who borrowed their grandfathers' shotguns to do target practice in the Chalchihuapan ravine; their hair was just a little long, their pants a little dirty, and their idea of justice included killing a few thousand people to atone for centuries of ignominy.

He doesn't talk about it much, but from certain things my mother let slip when she was still living with us, I've managed to gather that two of his comrades were disappeared, another spent a few years in prison, while, on the other hand, nothing happened to Dad. When, as a teenager, I told Erre all this he came to the rather hasty conclusion that in order to get away scot-free, the old man must have been a government informer, but I suspect that in fact his innate cowardice kept him, by the grace of Marx, slightly on the margins of direct action and more on the side of convoluted revolutionary debate (a practice he still enjoys, now on the telephone, when he's had a few too many drinks).

First the university and then blindness took the edge off his contentious nature, and it's only when he's arguing with me (usually over nothing at all) that I begin to fear muscle memory will come to his aid and he'll beat me to a pulp or dust off an old revolver and point it at the area of shadow from which my screams are coming, brandishing his weapon with the same determination he once employed to defend Rosa Luxemburg while a wounded comrade in arms was bleeding to death at his feet in a garage in Xochitepec.

Fortunately, things have never gone that far. Once or twice, I had to seek asylum in Erre's apartment in Mexico City until the old man cooled off, but that was all. Our reconciliations tend to include tequila, hugs, the odd tear, and a bunch of bilateral agreements: I'll wash the dishes more often and he won't demand that I drive him wherever he wants at the very moment he thinks of it (for example, to check if some botanera he used to frequent in the nineties is still there, as he did not long ago). Then our routine returns to its natural course: he retires to his office and I go to my bedroom, and although our tastes in music couldn't be farther apart, we tolerate each other's noise in the neutral spaces of the dining and living rooms, where we occasionally coincide, cordially ignoring each other, just as the chords of the Latin jazz he likes coexist with the raging guitar solos of my music.

Lately, since the wildfires started, we've been spending more time together. Our shared wonder at the fragility of the world leads us to make coffee after coffee, staring into space and musing that "it's all gone to blazes," an expression he taught me when I was small and that functions as a kind of parent-child mantra. The echo of my own pessimism in his fatalism offers a modicum of relief, just enough to see us through to the next cup of strong coffee.

The city my father lives in isn't exactly Cuernavaca, it's more like a palimpsest of personal and collective stories that occupy the space of Cuernavaca. As his blindness advanced and the outlines of things blurred until the things themselves vanished, a mirage rich in detail replaced cars and buildings with temples, patches of pre-Hispanic times, plus the cantinas of his youth, so that sometimes, as he's sipping his coffee, Dad says things like: Don Hernán Cortés had his sugarcane mill nearby; right here in Tlaltenango. And then, as if speaking of a recent past he himself had experienced, he goes on to tell me about the extractive logging process Cortés set up in Santa María Ahuacatitlán, somewhere around 1500, to make the machinery for his mill. Then he pauses and it's clear that the unstable time machine in his head has randomly switched again and, in the most natural manner imaginable, he adds: And in the eighties, a girlfriend of mine lived here, just behind us. We nicknamed her Floating Garden because she always had two or three crates of fruit in her Beetle, mostly chayote; heaven knows why.

In my view, the old man's historian's compulsion is not so much a professional defect as an evasive strategy: time stretches back to the past like a wall that extends up a humid, benevolent elevation with creeks and bottomless caves. In terms of the future, however, that wall passes through the flames. But that metaphor is in fact traitorous, an oversimplification my father rejects. For him, time isn't that line dotted with events that we were made to draw in elementary school, but a monolithic, all-inclusive presence. And that's why Hernán Cortés and Floating Garden greet each other as they cross Avenida Emiliano Zapata, a hundred and fifty meters from where my father, locked in his office and his blindness, laughs aloud as he learns to read Braille with the help of "Snow White and the Seven Dwarfs."

I dislike having to leave the house. Dad's old Chevy—which is now mine but rarely used—makes a horrible noise every time I start the engine, a short screech like a dentist's drill. And, what's more, I hate driving, hate feeling exposed to the ill humor of strangers and to my own anxieties, forming a lump in the center of my chest the instant my sweating hands grip the wheel.

And public transport is no better. The bus drivers on the Rutas are wary of my tattoos and, with shocking frequency, ask an officer to come aboard to search me when they stop at traffic signals, thinking I'm a thief.

I could, I guess, get around in cabs, and I sometimes do, but after a certain hour I'm scared of being kidnapped and disappeared, of my father having to report the case to the police and deal with the local tabloid press until, three months on, they find my body, or what's left of it, in a ditch by the roadside somewhere near Jojutla.

As a result, I only ever go out when absolutely necessary or when, after a long stretch of frequent disputes with my father, I feel the need to have an odd number of beers with Natalia in the unsightly, pretentious house where she lives with that cretin Argoitia. That's exactly what I did yesterday.

Even though we've known each other for twenty years, Natalia is still capable of surprising me. We've spent umpteen nights together, drinking beers, chatting, and making plans we never carry out, but despite that intense complicity, there's always something about her that escapes me; a musical box with a small mechanical bird singing a captivating tune in the inaccessible core of her personality. Her songs are sometimes sad; boleros of female laments that trickle down the adobe walls. But she also has wrathful tunes capable of devouring everything that crosses their path, like the flames of the wildfires wreaking havoc a few kilometers from her home.

In addition to that unpredictability, Natalia has a repetitive, almost ritual side to her personality. As I've known her for so long, I can safely say that part of her—made up of small backyard offerings and homespun miracles—has always been immutable, like an archaic alphabet of her psyche—a combination of symbols that, while limited in scope, are adequate for expressing a torrid, exuberant mythology, abounding with vices and plants.

When I visited yesterday, she didn't seem quite herself, as though possessed by a strange silence, always just about to express what is going on in her head but then thinking the better of it after a couple of words, like a doctor afraid to tell a patient they have only two months left to live and who, from sheer nerves, ends up talking about the weather. So I talked a lot to fill the lulls in her mood with everything I've been thinking about in the last two weeks but haven't been able to share with anyone. (Among other things, that I'm tempted to believe the theory that Cuernavaca's water has hallucinogenic properties; I read about it on a Reddit thread at three o'clock on Monday morning while I was snacking on Maria cookies with jam.)

I sometimes start to tell Dad about the waves of looting that have broken out in several cities across the world, the growing sensation that something is on the verge of collapse, but he doesn't seem particularly interested. He tells me that everything he needs to know is in his history books or the children's books I bought him to learn Braille. He says he could produce something identical to the present with a precise combination of what happened here, in a radius of two kilometers, from October to December 1560, and the final scenes of "Little Red Riding Hood," and that, moreover, he suspects the possible solutions to the problems of the present are somewhere in the past, and that those solutions, which for centuries were common knowledge, were often buried under the mire of some war and the shit of some fever. Only those who don't fear getting their hands a little dirty, he concludes, will have access to those bygone truths.

Then he takes out the pack of unfiltered Delicados he always has in his shirt pocket and puts a cigarette to his lips, holds it between his stained teeth, and, with the angular gesture of a figure in a Picasso painting I've seen innumerable times since childhood, tilts his head to one side to bring the lighter to the unsteady tip of the cigarette. For an instant, the flame illuminates his white corneas and then I understand that Dad is a sort of oracle, so disillusioned by the future he foresees that he's decided to completely ignore it, like a natural baritone who is forced to sing in another vocal range. He makes himself sing the song of the past, and lives there like a hibernating squirrel with everything he needs, never having to poke his nose out into the inclement present.

Not long ago, for instance, while we were eating a disgusting casserole I'd prepared, and which he angrily complained about for days afterward, my father told me—yet again—about the pre-Hispanic garden in Oaxtepec, of which Cortés gave a detailed description in his letters. But on this occasion, when I heard about the crystalline pools, the ancient Montezuma cypresses, and the brightly colored quetzals, I understood that the garden wasn't just another piece of historical data my father treasures and keeps scrupulously polished, but a real, wild, lush garden that appeared before his useless eyes whenever he called it up: an image more complete and vivid than the wildfires, the looting, and the multitudinous religious services occurring nowadays around the territory of Morelos State—the same territory to which my father still refers as the Tierra Caliente, as if he were living in the colonial era.

Growing up hearing those stories had led me to infer a dense undergrowth behind the visible: I very soon discovered that the reality offered to the senses—and this is at the heart of my belief systems—is scarcely the bush and definitely not the predator hidden behind it. Everything contains the seed of its own destruction. And that's why I tell Natalia that I'm an animist: the soul is my name for that potential for dissolution that beats within the heart of all things that exist.

My fascination with conspiracy theories springs from the same source. There's something comforting in assuming an order, a meaning, even a guilty party hiding behind the visible that is lying in wait and organizing things. But I have ambiguous feelings here, just as I do about horoscopes and some of the divinatory arts: I believe and I don't believe; at times I admit the idea of that order, and delight in its possibilities, but then I repent and become the most rational of cynics—or the most cynical of rationalists. During the moments when I succumb to the magical or conspiratorial explanation, everything suddenly seems to fall into line: Erre's pain is the fruit of a moral fault, for example; the result of a karma thirsting for equilibrium making its presence felt by fucking up his joints. But then I backtrack: Erre's pain is a matter of meaningless chance, as though he'd received a whack from the walking stick of some silly old codger while crossing one of the stinking streets behind the market on his way home. An accident, just like any other, possibly unavoidable and with no reason for its occurrence.

The same is true of my father's blindness: when I'm smoking pot and allow myself to be suffused by the mental murkiness that makes people say things like "everything is connected," I blame my father for being blind just as I blame him for being alone. I tell myself that he may in fact have betrayed his comrades in arms in his youth by informing on them to the police, and the shadow that has invaded his vision first invaded his soul, like a moral cancer silently eating away its core. But then I look out the window and see one of the stray cats that prowl the neighborhood, offered food in some houses and abuse in many others, and it seems idiotic to attribute his fate to some kind of law or a particular interest on the part of the universe in fucking up his life, and I see that my father is like that cat: it received food for a few years, followed by the harsh but random kick in the ass of fate, without any need to establish a pattern or a logic in the affair. I try not to hurt anyone and have relationships with only three or four people, but there's no reason why I shouldn't, in a blink of the eye, find myself an amputee or a vegetable, without deserving or fearing it.

What happens is that, setting aside their truth value or convenience, conspiracy theory explanations have an aesthetic I find enthralling, the way other people get excited about uniforms or dancing champeta, I guess. A good conspiracy theory always has an appealingly kitsch side. The idea, for example, that a scientist in Morelos has discovered an element in the periodic table that is being used to keep the population of Cuernavaca half asleep and mindless makes me think of certain movies that were all the rage in the seventies. When I suspect that reality is imitating the tackiest of fiction, some sort of gland I imagine to be situated near my genitals activates and I feel an authentic shudder running down my spine.

•

At first, my father refused to accept what was happening to him and continued to drive the Chevy to the university each day, just as usual. But when he got home, there would be three new scratches on the door and the fender hanging at an angle. He told Mom and me that he needed to get stronger glasses but hadn't had time (despite the fact that we'd seen him sitting in his office every evening doing nothing). Mom never had much patience with him—with anyone, to be honest—but in those early days she agreed to drop him at the university, as it was on her way to work. For the return journey, Dad took the Ruta 13 or bummed a ride with a colleague who was taking his son to a taekwondo class near our house. But one day he got on the wrong bus and ended up in the CIVAC industrial park; he rang Mom and the two of us drove there to find him. That image is stamped in my memory: my father standing on a corner, under one of those torrential rainstorms we used to have at the turn of the century, without making the slightest effort to take shelter. Mom pulled over, and when I wound down the window, I was able to see his face more clearly; his features seemed smudged by rain and confusion. He didn't look directly at me, and I suspect that by then he couldn't see much anyway, because it wasn't until he heard my voice that he sketched what I guess was meant to be a smile and stretched out his hand, like a baby trying to get hold of a sippy cup. It took him a second or two to find the door handle and then get in, with my mom scolding him for having stood there like a numbskull—her words—in the downpour.

The following day, he finally agreed to see a specialist,

although he had to wait two months for his first appointment because there was only one ophthalmologist in Cuernavaca whose fees were covered by his insurance policy and Dad refused to fork out four hundred pesos to see another. During those two months his symptoms grew more severe. He'd ask me to switch on the light in the living room (already on) or read him the politics section of the newspaper, and I, almost unconsciously, took on the role of a seeing-eye dog and wound up progressively sorting out his problems. Mom was often working late at that time, or so she said. We learned afterward that she wasn't coming straight home: she'd go to see a movie on her own at seven o'clock or sit on a café terrace downtown to drink rum cocktails until she felt drunk enough to deal with her blind husband and teenage son.

But the appearance of Dr. Ángel Mendiola on the scene signified a marked improvement, if not for my father's vision, at least for the atmosphere at home. The ophthalmologist was a snake charmer: he promised Dad that within six months he'd be seeing better than ever, said he'd have him included in a medical trial that would give him access to experimental, first-world treatment, and claimed that a regime of alarmingly simple optic nerve exercises would gradually help him to recoup the visual territory he'd lost.

Dad put every crumb of his faith in those promises. He'd spend the mornings raising his eyes or looking sideways at a light bulb for hours until he got a headache. On Sundays, he'd sit at the dining table and fill his pill organizer with all the tablets the doctor gave him, the overwhelming majority of which were simple supplements and antioxidants. In the meantime, behind my father's back (or rather, before his very eyes, because by then he couldn't see anything), Mom traded in alcoholism and cinema-going for a friendship, and later, an affair with Dr. Mendiola, who used to make appointments with her in his office on the pretext of receiving reports on my father's—his patient's—progress.

If I'd spent more time at home in those days, I'm sure I'd have noticed it: happiness suited my mother like a borrowed dress that wasn't quite her style. But I was in my second year of high school and was spending all my spare time trying out different color hair dyes and drinking with Natalia and Erre in Plazuela del Zacate. Apart from when I was reading the paper to my father and helping him to book a cab (he was still giving classes), I didn't pass much time in the house, which seemed a far too hegemonic and normal space in which to squander the nectar of my originality.

Just before the summer vacation that year, Natalia and I discovered a vacant lot not far from the Arcadia, whose crumbling wall was like an invitation to enter. I don't know exactly how big it was, but we used to call it the "hectare plot" because that size seemed appropriate. On the other side of the wall was a lush forest of bamboo, planted in serried ranks. I sometimes went there to walk with Natalia and Erre and we'd each make our way along a different row at our own pace. We'd chat as we moved closer and apart between the perfectly vertical bamboos, following one another's progress through the foliage of an unreal landscape that heightened the effects of the marijuana. The bamboo forest came to an abrupt halt farther along and the land dropped steeply. There was also a ruined house, a one-story affair with thick walls where the people who entered the lot took a shit, and left condoms or other mementos. If you continued walking beyond the ruins, you reached a stinking stream and a sort of waterfall—equally malodorous—where we'd sometimes sit to drink beer and throw stones into the water.

We started going to the hectare plot every day after school and before Natalia's dance class. It wasn't a particularly pretty place, but it was more or less ours, although we did sometimes come across teenagers from a nearby technical high school, smoking crack in the ruins or having fistfights among the bamboo. That year, Erre flunked two subjects, and Natalia and I were helping him revise for the retakes. Those two were dating then, but it didn't last: that was the summer they went to Oaxaca together and came back almost hating each other, as often happens with first loves.

But even when our small gang of callow fugitives broke up—all gangs of adolescents are destined to form and then separate—the vacant bamboo lot remained as an unspoiled symbol of that lost unity, that original community to which we will always secretly belong, like people standing before a mirror to put on the uniform of a defeated army in the safety and sadness of their homes; like people singing the national anthem of a defunct country in the shower. And in fact the only community that could ever replace that other, defeated one would be the family, but we are all denied the possibility of forming a family because our only way of being in the world is as unwilling offspring, and when our parents die, and with them our fractured identities, we'll be white dwarfs, silent, collapsed stars wandering through the cosmos with neither light nor system.

One evening around that time—when, for better or worse, I locate the origin of my adult personality—Erre and I went to the hectare plot alone. We spent a while chatting about nothing in particular, but he was in a weird mood, evasive, as though keeping a secret he didn't want to offload. We were sitting on a small mound between two rows of bamboo, resting against a rock. I took advantage of an awkward silence to look up and was lost to the world, watching the slow dance of the bamboo, bowing slightly in the wind, like a crowd of Buddhist monks greeting one another across a square. After a time, as though we were already talking about it, Erre blurted out: I really like Natalia. I immediately knew what he was getting at (that the equilateral triangle of our relationship had become more isosceles, with those two moving closer while I was sinking farther and farther from the base), but I played the moron: I really like her too, I said, that's why she's our friend, right? Erre smiled, like he was letting me know he wasn't buying that: You know what I mean; it's getting serious, I think she's the one for me. That expression sounded naive, worthy of the most stupid characters at the Arcadia: hominids who washed the car every weekend and announced, without a trace of self-consciousness, that when they graduated they were going to study business administration at some private college with a questionable academic record. Naturally, I didn't say that to Erre; I didn't want to make him mad. Instead, I put a hand on his thigh, leaned in, and kissed his neck. Erre initially drew back a little, the way the leaves of a touch-me-not mimosa do on contact, but then he turned and kissed me on the mouth. Through the warm fabric of his black jeans, I felt his dick hardening. I massaged it lightly as the kiss went on and then opened his zipper. He lay back on the ground, by the rock, in a position that didn't look too comfortable. I sucked him off slowly until he came in my mouth.

I remember thinking that his come tasted like sweet granadilla, a fruit I'd once sampled in a market, whose seed-filled flesh seemed somehow over the top, as if there were something unidentifiable in the flavor—beyond the lingering aftertaste of cold coins. Erre pulled up his pants and we leaned back against the rock—him with dirt in his hair and on his clothes, me with a sudden craving for beer. I didn't say anything because I thought Erre seemed distant. He'd perhaps been lost to the world too, watching the movement of the bamboo while I was doing my thing. He'd perhaps discovered some profound truth about himself in that delicate dance and needed to be alone to digest it. But most likely, I thought, he was frightened by his own desire—that thousand-headed hydra, that god capable of assuming any form: from the vulnerable fawn to the ancient cypress; I don't think it was guilt—that wasn't something Erre tended to suffer—just the sheer terror of seeing the boundless hunger, the dizzyingly vast ocean of his desire.

We walked back to the wall in silence and waved goodbye with calculated indifference once we were outside the hectare plot.

The following morning, in school, Erre's attitude to me was still reserved. He joined a rowdy mob of dudes playing soccer in the yard, like he needed to reaffirm his manhood in a group, under the aegis of the violence of others. Natalia and I reacted to that unheard-of betrayal by going off to smoke in a quiet cul-de-sac near the school with a traffic circle at the far end containing a flamboyant tree that in my memory is always in bloom. But on our way we saw another tree, a palm, with its crown in flames. Apparently, a tangle of utility cables had shorted and set fire to it. The palm was like a giant torch signaling some religious event, standing alone, burning in the middle of the street, as combustible as any of us. Natalia and I watched it for a while, each thinking our own thoughts, with the same expression of stunned fascination on our faces.

I'm not sure why, but that spectacle made me ask Natalia what she was thinking of doing when we finished high school. I'd like to go to Europe, she said, to study choreography in Holland or at a university I've found in Prague. The prospect of Natalia disappearing all too soon from my life was awful, I felt part of a hillside breaking off close to my lungs and coughed a few times. And do you think Erre will go with you? I asked when I was able to talk again. She said she had no idea, said she liked dating Erre and they were thinking of taking a trip to Oaxaca together, but sometimes she didn't quite understand him. And then she added: He's not like you, Conejo, or like me either; we can chat by telepathy, but Erre can't even hear his own thoughts. That felt like a cruel thing to say, but it was true: Erre's head seemed to be surrounded by an invisible swarm most of the time, like a cloud of white noise.

A fire truck arrived to deal with the palm tree, but it turned out the firefighters had forgotten to fill the tank and there was no water, so they stood beside us, looking on. I imagined that together we formed a tribe of Paleolithic humans dazzled by a palm tree struck by lightning. Night would soon fall and some of us would be devoured by predators.

Picking up where I'd left off with Natalia, I said: I don't always understand him either. It's like he suddenly becomes different from himself; he has a kaleidoscopic personality. Natalia laughed at that image and put her arm around my shoulder, saying, Smartass: One day we'll both be famous, even if it's against your will. Famous? Sure, whatever, I retorted, and we started pushing each other in a pretense of roughness. We walked back to school and went to the cafeteria; we had a few minutes spare before the next class. I remember that it was hot, though not as hot as now. The Casino de la Selva hadn't yet been demolished and its trees made the whole neighborhood pleasantly humid.

That same day, after class, I looked around for Natalia and Erre in the chaos of the schoolyard, but they had already left. And for the first time I felt that the golden thread linking our destinies for just over a year—at that time of our lives, a geological period—had snapped.

What we are left with are broken families, blind or aging parents, the resigned company of the people who gave life to us and then got fed up with us, but who tolerate us the way you tolerate a bad leg that hurts when it rains. We're their twisted offshoots, their walking, talking extensions, their bothersome shadows.

On certain evenings, darkened by smoke, in a sort of Marxist sequel, Dad recovers a form of blind optimism based on the belief that, due to its dialectic structure, history is advancing without fail in the right direction toward its own dissolution in a workers' paradise. All this, he tells me—with a gesture that takes in the neighborhood, the city, the whole world—is basically a backward step necessary for advancement: conflict will bring about progress. But his conviction falters on the final syllable of each word, spoken more quietly, as though at heart he were embarrassed by his short outburst. After those rare episodes of optimism, he slowly returns to his habitual fatalism. A few hours of silence in the half-light of the living room, drinking one cup of coffee after another, bring him back to the anguish of the present, which merges with the disdain of the prophet who sees—or in this case, hears—the world go up in flames, just as he'd predicted.

Today I've witnessed him moving along that route from blind confidence in the working class's success in the struggle to desolate eight-o'clock weariness, when he's overcome by hunger for his dinner and the certainty that it's all going to blazes.

But now, without warning, he's emerging from that pool of caffeine-fueled anguish with a smile lighting up his face and a redemptive idea: We have to take a trip, he tells me, almost shouting. First thing tomorrow. He says he wants to go to the coast, to hear the sea. I reply that there's no need to go anywhere: I can play the sound of the sea through those good-quality speakers I gave him a few years back, the last time I had a steady job. It'll sound better through the speakers than in person, I tell him, and you won't have to put up with all that sand in your butt crack or the stink of coconut-oil sunblock, or have to listen to Chilangos playing flag football and throwing up by the palm-leaf beach umbrella. And anyway, I add, I don't think the car is up to it: we'll be left high and dry in some one-horse town in Chilpancingo with two OXXOs and forty Lobo pickups, at the mercy of the sun and organized crime. But Dad isn't giving up that easily: I want to say goodbye, I don't have much time left; I don't think I'll ever visit the sea again. We can go tomorrow and come back on Monday, I'll pay, I've got a little stash tucked away. And, he rounds off, Cuernavaca is awful these days, with all these wildfires, and anyway, you don't do a fucking thing except lounge about in your bedroom smoking pot. I might be blind but I'm not stupid. His insistence has me tearing my hair out so, to get him off my back, I say we can go to the coast for a couple of days but I can't do that weekend: it's the first night of Natalia's performance and she'll never forgive me if I miss it.

To my surprise, Dad quits talking about the sea and asks about my friend. Is she still living with that man? Yes, I reply, she's still with Argoitia: he's a schmuck (I read the word in a colloquial translation yesterday and have been wanting to use it all day). But I have the feeling she's going to ditch him; she doesn't seem as head over heels as she was at first. Plus, Erre's back and I'm hoping those two will make up; I mean, it's been years. Then, in a tone I want to sound hopeful, I add: Who knows, they might get together again and have a kid. Dad laughs and I find his coffee-stained teeth slightly repulsive. He says: You ought to be on the lookout for a woman for yourself, not for your friend. A woman or a man, I quip, but he pretends not to hear. We sit in silence for a time and I wonder how Natalia's doing. It's just one day until her performance and she still hasn't told me much about it. When I call, she seems distracted; she hangs up abruptly without even saying goodbye, my SMSs appear to be read but either she doesn't reply or sends quotations from whatever she's reading just then: long paragraphs about a proto-hippy choreographer and a German psychiatrist who lived a century ago.

Erre, for his part, arranged to come around today after lunch but stood me up. Not that we had any big plans: I'd put three beers in the fridge and I wanted to play him an album by a group from Yautepec with a girl shouting herself hoarse rapping poems about ovarian pain.

I'm a bit worried about Erre. He was a mess the last time he came here. In addition to his confusion about what day it is, I've noticed that he forgets lots of other things. He asked if Dad was still teaching, when he knows well he retired years ago.

There's something depressing about hanging out with people who've known you forever. They always expect you to be the same as you were before, to embody that person preserved in the formaldehyde of the memory, to whom they have an inalienable lifetime right. Erre disappeared off the scene for years, only popping up in my life for the occasional phone call or short visit, and now he's back and comes around whenever he feels like it, expecting me to be here and ready to listen to him talking over and over about his pain and his divorce, as though he's never left. And, to be honest, I expect a degree of coherence from him too: I expect that he never changes beyond recognition, that he laughs at the same jokes and allows the same caresses with the awkward reluctance of his hard-ons when I run my fingers through his tousled hair, with that mix of tenderness and irony that characterizes the love of childhood friendships. But maybe it would be better not to know him, to ask more often about his fears and traumas, as if we'd never danced until dawn in some cantina with a sticky floor.

While I'm getting ready to go to Natalia's event, I note that my pulse is accelerated. Possibly, I think, because I have to drive downtown and return after dark—something I've managed to avoid for ages. Or more likely it's my damned empathy setting my nerves on edge: I imagine how Natalia's feeling and, in a flash, my vital signs are copying that state, like a person yawning when they see someone else yawn. I know she must be nervous too, even if she pretends otherwise, even if she plays the tough guy and makes out that nothing in this small town can really affect her.

I send a message to Erre, who's still not showing signs of life. He's probably back in Mexico City, I think, dealing with unemployment and the wide world of possibilities open to him; he must be making one last desperate effort to save his marriage and return to the solace of normality: to the inertia of adult life, the steady, full-time job, the occasional affair, maybe even children. He came to Cuernavaca, took one look at me—condemned to being my father's caretaker, living a vicarious historical existence through his stories—and repented all his decisions. He perhaps wanted to take his chances with the future, whatever it was. As if such a thing existed.

Since I don't have any clothes suitable for the occasion, I ask Dad if I can borrow the sky-blue guayabera with a Mao collar he bought in Veracruz back in the nineties, during the only family holiday I remember from childhood. Apart from the smell of mothballs, it's in good condition, not a thread out of place.

My father says: Don't even think of wearing it with those flea-infested jeans of yours; I'll lend you my pleated pants, they must be here somewhere in the closet. And then after a pause: Apologize to Natalia for me, but modern dance isn't my thing. And he accompanies his joke with an ironic smile that quickly fades.

I check the clock: it's early yet. I change and leave the house. The infernal noise the Chevy makes when I start up the engine puts me on the alert.

I feel slightly ridiculous dressed this way, in this elegant, slightly loose-fitting attire of thirty years ago, driving a car that makes an awful din when you start it up and whose bodywork also shows evidence of the cruel passage of time.

The sun is a little less strong now, but the violet hues of the sky show a high concentration of particulate matter. I'd like to be able to say that, given the environmental conditions, I'm surprised Natalia's event is still going ahead but the truth is that nothing, or very little, surprises me these days. We've all become accustomed to the stories of people being unable to breathe and asthmatics dropping like flies while tongues of fire lick every corner of the state.

During a long wait at a set of traffic lights, I call Erre, but he's not answering. I leave a voicemail asking, yet again, if I'll see him in the Jardín Borda, but I'm beginning to suspect I won't. In an act of supreme desperation, he returned to Cuernavaca, slept with Natalia, came around to my place to make eyes at me, and then, as usual, took to his heels.

The labyrinthine streets of downtown Cuernavaca and the noise of car horns leave my nerves like stalactites or fragile icicles about to break off and slit my throat. I decide to put the Chevy in a parking lot for fear of someone breaking the windows to steal the dust, the seats, and the dirty, sweat-laden air in the interior.

As I drop off the keys, I ask what time they close, but the assistants just grunt—their red-slash mouths in ash-stained faces—and point to a sign saying "Open 24 Hours."

I weave through the street vendors who, despite all attempts by the municipal administration, are everywhere, hawking Chinese household air purifiers with PM2.5 filters, or plastic and wooden back scratchers, or T-shirts with pictures of a drug baron taken out ten years ago in the beautiful, crowded streets of this very city.

Only when I'm crossing the Jardín Juárez does the ambience of the city change: the vendors are replaced by gringo photographers, attracted like flies by the modest ending of our world; hunger strikers demonstrating in front of the Palacio de Gobierno carrying placards complaining about the wildfires in their communities; flocks of evangelists handing out flyers proclaiming the good news that everything—surprise, surprise—will soon be fine: the in-your-face coming of the Lord.

As I'm passing the cathedral, I remember, as I always do, Dad's stories about Méndez Arceo, the Red Bishop, who preached socialism from the pulpit in the sixties and seventies. According to those tales—possibly invented by my father, I'm not sure—the bishop was a staunch defender of the Latin American guerrillas of those decades, to the extent of, on more than one occasion, allowing them to use the cathedral's secret tunnels (according to some people, they connect with the Jardín Borda, as Maximilian had them dug as a possible escape route) to hide comrades pursued by a variety of organizations. One time, said Dad—by then blind and trapped in his memory—the bishop told us that if we wanted to hide weapons in the sacristy, God wouldn't object, but the truth is we only had two old revolvers back then, and we left them with Toña, a woman who'd taken refuge in Mexico during the Spanish Civil War and whose brother was an anarchist belonging to the Durruti Column. She had a place selling paella on the road to Teopanzolco, right by the pyramid—it isn't exactly a pyramid, just the memory of one: the suggestion of a ruined city.

The Red Bishop, or my remembrance of the tale my father

tells of him—the evocation of those secret tunnels that populate rumors, as happens in so many other cities, and supposedly link the mansions downtown—by some fluke of the memory made me think of a book Dad was always referring to about five years ago: *In the Shadow of the Peaks*, by Stata B. Couch. Based on what I managed to deduce from my dad's monologues (he was drinking a lot around then and at times was pretty incomprehensible), it was a romantic pulp novel set in Cuernavaca in 1909, in which an enigmatic foreign woman is drugged with opium and taken to one of those legendary tunnels. And as I recall that book—which I never read but heard more than enough about—it occurs to me that it would be fucking marvelous if, in some kind of archaeological fit, Natalia were to include those hidden tunnels in her dance: so the whole audience, all in their best duds—including me in my spotless sky-blue guayabera—was made to walk through those precarious, moldy tunnels smelling of bird shit and other disgusting things, chasing naked dancers who are writhing in the slime like mutant axolotls, turning their tensed faces or twisted limbs toward the dim beam of a flashlight. This image—even more, I'd say this vision—of Natalia's choreography cheers me up, so I buy an elote to eat before the function starts, and I ask the aid of my patron saint—the Red Bishop of Cuernavaca, Méndez Arceo—in preventing the mayo, grated cheese, and salsa—the mild one—from dripping onto the sky-blue guayabera because, while Dad is blind and might not notice the stain, the thought of having to spend two hours with a splotch on my shirt, surrounded by the bunch of jerks and wimps that frequent such events, already makes me feel like going back home to my bedroom to drink beer, take drugs, and later tell Natalia that I sat through the whole performance but left straight afterward, that it was sublime, overflowing with grace and violence. But, luckily, the mayo stays on the corn and I proudly show my ticket at the entrance to the Jardín Borda, walk through the dried-out trees to the lakeside stage, and sit at one end of a row, near the exit, to observe the strange rituals of this cultured public.

Maximilian of Hapsburg—or Mexico—became sterile, and made his wife, Carlota of Belgium, sterile too due to a venereal disease contracted in an African brothel. (That's probably not how it went, but it's my preferred version of the story, constructed from snippets of conversations with my father over tequila and the very little I've retained from history classes in the Arcadia.) The childless couple ended up living out their days in the Borda—he eventually faced a firing squad, she went mad years later—and on the rare occasions when I visit, I imagine them here, now, eating nisperos on these same seats, contemplating the scene of our destruction, and, like all good misplaced Europeans, stubbornly clinging to a senseless erotico-imperial fantasy.

And that's how I am too, childless and slightly out of place in my sky-blue guayabera, waiting for Natalia's work to start—it's half an hour late: still within the normal limits for this neck of the woods—sitting seven rows behind a government official—the undersecretary for culture, I think—whose gummy smile when she poses for the cameras of the social pages I honestly swear dazzles me, to the extent that I'm afraid I'll go blind too, as though instead of sparkling gums and teeth, I'd viewed . . . I don't know . . . a total eclipse of the sun.

Time goes on passing—always does, I guess—and the impatient official calls a flunky, who in turn calls another, who leads the old, decaying Argoitia to the official, and I overhear that something must have gone wrong. Natalia left for the event long before he did, says Argoitia, it's not like her to be late, "especially when she's so pleased about having the premiere in the historic Jardín Borda."

I'm a little worried. I check my phone to see if there's a message from her—Natalia—but no, nothing. So I send her one ("everything ok? heightening the excitement for your triumphal entrance? you come in a horse and carriage?") but she doesn't read it, and more time passes and she still hasn't read it, and the official with the sparkling gums decides she's fulfilled her duty by smiling for the social pages, grabs her things, calls her flunkies (one flunky who calls another), and leaves. Argoitia is pacing up and down like a caged tiger, nervous that Natalia might not show up, and his nervousness becomes a rumor that gathers speed and circulates among the frustrated audience (women with their hair in updos, teenagers who've been dragged along and are now immersed in their mobile phones): It's not only Natalia who hasn't turned up, they comment, her dancers aren't here either. That's to say, absolutely nothing and nobody, and if you ask me, there's no never, much less a forever. People are fidgeting in their seats. Some stand up to stretch their legs; others head for a café. An hour overdue. As jittery as a cokehead, I check my phone every two minutes to see if Natalia has read my message, but it's just nothing and more nothing, and I'm left in astonished nothingness, planted like a flowerpot while the lakeside stage and the garden slowly empty.

Only Argoitia and I remain, looking at each other from afar without daring to speak, and it's darker now and we're alone, in the middle of that nothingness, both waiting for some improbable answer—any answer—that isn't coming. The stage has no curtain, but if it did, the crimson velvet would flood everything like blood, advising us that maybe, I don't know, it's time for us to go. Time for the two of us to get the fuck out.

As we make for the exit, we fall into step by a fountain and Argoitia asks me, in that slurry, sordid voice of his, if I (he uses my name) have heard anything from my friend and I say no, that nothing like this has ever happened before. I tell him I'd arranged to meet her and Erre, but neither turned up. And the shadow of irate jealousy darkens the face of the great painter and I give myself two pats on the back: first because it's always lovely to hurt Argoitia, and then because Natalia fucked all of us up, and nobody is absent from that *all of us*, except maybe Erre, who might—or might not—be with her.

The aged painter and I say goodbye with a nod that really means, "let me know if you hear anything" but also hides a "go fuck yourself." He walks to his car without, of course, offering me a ride; I retrace my route: I pass the cathedral—so poorly renovated that it would have been better to let the pigeon shit finish it off—and sit on the terrace of a nearby café to have a beer.

I order, the beer comes, but I don't have a chance to drink it because, just as I'm about to take my first sip, some guy comes along the street making the weirdest movements, writhing, jumping and prancing, throwing his whole body onto the flagstones time after time, and then the next thing I know he's irrupting onto the terrace where I'm sitting, knocking over everything in his path: he bangs into seats and spills my beer when he hits the legs of the plastic table, kicks the waiter, and topples like a tree trunk onto the hot meal of a whole family—they stare in horror and the grandmother screams. Someone—the manager, a security guard, I'm not sure—comes out and attempts to grab him and muscle him back into the street, but at the first touch the guy—the erratic dancer—stands upright again and nimbly runs off, his forehead bleeding and with a smile as pure and bright as summer on his face, leaving the rest of us dumbstruck, gaping like idiots. Someone else—a waiter, a security guard—runs up the street to notify the patrol that's normally stationed on the corner of Avenida Morelos, but soon returns, saying they aren't there, there are no police anywhere, and no one is answering the emergency number. And while a small group of self-appointed leaders discuss the best course of action (whether to chase the bum, to beat him up), and before the grandmother can recover from her shock, a second dancer—this time a woman—appears on the terrace, and then a third and a fourth: a troupe of clowns in civilian dress, with unhinged expressions, kicking whatever piece of furniture they encounter in their improvised dance.

One of the dancers has her boobs hanging out, another is very short and wears the malignant expression of clowns in old movies. And we're all so astounded and upset that we get out fast so as not to find ourselves in the path of a phenomenon that seems almost climatic, as though a whirlwind had suddenly blown up and was carrying away all our certainties and leaving, in part exchange, a miserable hoax: shattered glasses, shattered shards of glasses strewn everywhere; bloodied tablecloths and something that looks like shit in the turnups of the pants of a man who is shouting like one possessed: Sons of bitches! Sons of bitches!

One piece of collateral damage of the situation is that my phone is broken. Someone stepped on it or threw it to the ground, but whatever, it's busted, unusable. I leave it there and head for my car. Something is going on. Most likely the poison the authorities have been putting in the water has finally taken effect and is sending us all crazy. Or more likely still, the ash from the multiple wildfires is stopping oxygen getting through to people's gray matter and they're starting to do dumb stuff, kicking everything in sight like in the punk concert I went to in Pachuca ten years ago that ended with a toll of three dead. Who knows, but something is going on and I need to check my dad is safe.

There are no cars on the avenue: a crowd of gawkers have taken over the streets, shouting or trying—vainly—to use their telephones. People are behaving like a flock of parrots at sundown: they fly back and forth in formation, squawking loudly, and then they change their minds and follow another bird going in the opposite direction. A child of about seven wearing the—old and faded—T-shirt of the now defunct soccer team Colibríes de Cuernavaca stands in the middle of the throng looking drowsily at the sky, as though expecting a miracle, and the miracle appears in the form of a microbus going the wrong way down the street and wipes him out.

I've hardly slept these last five days. Sometimes, around noon, I doze at the table and Dad just sits there, silently keeping me company, until I wake after a few minutes. Then later, in my bedroom, with my laptop on my knees, I drop off again for a while until the sound of a gunshot nearby wakes me, and I quickly open another tab to check for the latest news on TV or social media, as if some radical change could have occurred in the past five minutes. But everything is pretty much the same as before I fell asleep: there's a state of emergency and people are throwing themselves down in the street and suddenly can't stop prancing about and writhing until a) they die, b) they are killed, or c) their families pay a psychiatric response team to tackle them to the ground and administer an intramuscular sedative in the ass.

Natalia reemerged on the second day: she called our

landline—I'd forgotten we had one—to say she was fine and had gone to stay with her mother in Tepoztlán until things calmed down. I asked about Argoitia, but she didn't reply. Then, after a pause, she said: You know the outbreak had nothing to do with me, don't you? And I said: Yes, I know; it's a public health issue. She, again, made no reply, as though she were trying to figure out what I was referring to, so I added by way of explanation: It's an unpleasant coincidence that your dance performance and the start of this mayhem happened at the same time.

Naturally, to avoid mortifying her, I didn't say what I really thought: that her nasty trick of setting people to dance in the street had been the match that ignited the fire; that the collective psychosis in the city had been waiting for that spark to go off with a bang.

She asked after my dad and wanted to know if we had food in the house so we wouldn't need to go out. I told her we were okay, and that I'd gone to the OXXO that morning for groceries and to buy a disposable cell phone, and would try to stay indoors until the weekend now: You wouldn't believe how crazy people are acting, Natalia; right here in Tlaltenango, there are vigilante groups cracking down violently on any outbreak. They're armed with sticks and hammers and using them if you so much as scratch your shoulder because, they say, that's how it starts and then people begin jumping and kicking; seems to me there are as many victims of the cure as the illness itself.

Yeah, I saw that on the news, says Natalia in an absent tone, like her mind is on other things. We've had five days of this madness and she sounds as if she's bored with the whole affair, already knows the end of the story. She even goes so far as to change the subject, telling me she's glad she got out before the highways were closed because she wants to see if she can manage to go to Europe, where a foundation has offered her a half scholarship—the email had just arrived.

She asks—not getting her hopes up—if I have any spare dough to lend her for the flight, but I say no, tell her my dad is blind and I'm a freelancer; I still haven't been paid for several jobs and there have been a minimum of forty-seven deaths in Cuernavaca, plus the general panic and National Guard detachments patrolling the streets with high-caliber firearms. Natalia butts in: High-caliber fire charms? I love it. Firearms! I shout, and my voice sounds shriller than I expected. Firearms, I repeat more calmly. Doesn't sound like it bothers you much.

Natalia apologizes and explains that she's very tired, she hasn't been able to sleep for checking her phone constantly: she had to leave the bromeliads at Argoitia's and she's trying to hire someone to bring them to Tepoztlán, walking through the ravine to avoid the control posts. In a resigned voice—I'm assuming that it's impossible to talk to her about what's happening because the attraction her navel exercises on her eyes exceeds any other concern—I ask what she intends to do with the plants if she goes to Europe. I don't know, maybe take them with me, she responds, and I understand that she, too, must be a little overwhelmed by this end-of-the-world stuff. It gets to us all in different ways.

Dad, for his part, is melancholic. He keeps asking me to read him the news but then waves a hand to stop me: The truth is, I don't care, he says and descends into silence. I haven't heard him putting on music or laughing at his Braille children's books for days; he spends the evening like that, sitting silently in his armchair in the living room or in the comfortable chair in his office, with the lights out—of course, he never switches them on—like a shaman or a shadow fern.

Erre, on the other hand, hasn't gotten in touch.

I searched for his name in the lists of hospitalized people and deaths, but he must be among the disappeared; that list is always incomplete and has never been digitized. When I rang his parents' house, nobody picked up: I evaluated the risk of walking there but am afraid to go that far with all the episodes of police violence that are still being talked about, so I've done my best not to think any more about him for the moment. It will most likely turn out that he left the city with his parents as soon as he saw the scale of the ruckus. There are people who shelled out for a helicopter ride, and it wouldn't surprise me if Erre's father had dipped into his savings to get out of the mess.

I haven't even tried. I refuse to leave Cuernavaca for this. If I didn't go during the worst years of the war on drugs—assuming those years have now passed, as is so often claimed—I'm not leaving because a couple of hundred people have started dancing spasmodically in the street. Anyway, my bedroom window has bars: no one's going to dive in amid a hail of broken glass, with contorted features and kicking everything in sight, as they say happened in a house in Palmira due to an outbreak.

On news bulletins, in the opinion sections of papers, in the conversations echoing incredulously on every corner of the—devastated and hurting—city, the same explanations can be heard, at times contradictory and at others corroborative. No one has a clear timeline of the events but the experts—I flatter myself on being right in my first diagnosis—say that prolonged inhalation of carbon dioxide and the other toxic delicacies of the smoke from the wildfires triggered psychotic episodes in certain people who might—or might not—have a genetic predisposition.

On the other hand, in the darkest and most odiferous corners of the Web, where the craziest creatures thrive, and which I visit with morbid delight, they say that the city's water supply, as had been earlier claimed, has been contaminated for years (here, the general public is divided into those who believe this was intentional—"silly conspiracy theorists"—and those who think it was accidental—described as "simpletons" by the others). The oily evangelist Don Profeta, however, held a mass in a public space in Temixco to lay the blame on—naturally—the vampires of laicism, who lie in wait among the embers of now extinguished wildfires.

Other groups also use the situation to display their own agendas in the store window; here the guilty parties are: hydrocarbons, indigenous people, organized crime, environmentalists, and climate skeptics; drunks who flee to the hills pursued by their delirium tremens and accidentally set light to a blade of grass, thinking it's a cigarette; guardians of law and order who kidnap preadolescents under the influence of cocaine; Catholic priests who pass around the offertory box for those made homeless but squander their tithes on trans prostitutes; enraged campesinos who do their best to detain the boot of progress with the—egoistic!—aim of not being ground underfoot; citizens, in short, who never do enough for their neighbors, or always do too much—on this final point, no one agrees.

A scientific commission arrived in the city last night to investigate the events, but every single one of them has already been dismissed as incompetent by another group of scientists who reject their conclusions a priori. And given the resulting calm—of that fantastic canceling-out of all the opposites, that yin-yang of unleashed opinion—life goes on as before. There's still a slight smell of smoke, although it's gradually dispersing, and at night a few stars can be seen in the sky—timid twinkles no one notices, occupied as we are with more worldly things.

Now, at night, I jerk off and cry. Not necessarily at the same time, although that does sometimes happen. The pink dildo and a box of tissues, the computer like a sham lighthouse that causes shipwrecks, the books, magazines, and CDs—I hardly ever listen to them—the shirts, boxers, and frayed jeans watching me from the closet: everything around me has taken on a kind of sacred air, like a talisman that, when touched, protects against the return of misfortune.

The world is a bioluminescent beach, magnetized by dreams and defeat, but I prefer not to see it; rather, I choose to stay in my bedroom, eat rice with pink coloring, and drink a chard smoothie, spy on the debacle through the peephole of my convictions without really verifying them: I'm not interested in the flourishing conflict that sustains democracy, or the strident voices of leaders, or cat memes. What do interest me are microscopic love, comets, the persistent presence of beetles on the mosquito net, my dad's harsh voice when he says: Have you paid the property tax, you damned slacker? or, Your bedroom smells like manure, clean it, this instant.

Two weeks have gone by since the peak of the catastrophe, four days without a single incident. The national news bulletins have moved on to other issues and the locals are trying to find a "human angle," with pathetic results. They interview middle-aged women who lost children during the "kick dance," as someone christened it and everyone now calls it.

Erre still hasn't turned up.

Natalia's pretending nothing happened.

Dad's behaving like he's depressed.

Two neighbors were chatting outside, under the mango tree near my window. Lying on the floor by my bed, staring into space, I eavesdropped on their conversation. I could have gone to the window to see their faces, but I was transfixed by the flow of the conversation and was afraid they'd see me and stop. Their voices were so similar that I sometimes wondered if it wasn't in fact some crazy talking to herself, feigning that delirious dialogue. I don't remember the exact words, and my memory is undoubtedly filling a few gaps with inventions of its own, but even so, I'm leaving here a record of what I heard, as it seems like a fairly accurate barometer of the hype and rumors of these days.

"How did it start?"

"Just like this."

"Like what?"

"Like normal, like any old normal day. It was hot but you couldn't see the sun for all the smoke. Picture it: at around this time, someone is on the Ruta 3 in Santa María, near that former monastery where they say some monks went mad."

"I don't know it, but never mind. Go on."

"It isn't important. I don't even think it began in Santa María. It started everywhere at the same time. The point is that a number of people are on that bus, and a woman, traveling alone, gets up from her seat and falls in the aisle. The other passengers are startled."

"Wait a minute. So the woman is left lying there on the floor?"

"For a while, yes. But then she gets to her feet, all tense and stiff, and, pulling a face, she falls again. Talk about scary. One woman shouts: Help her! and in the back seats, two men look at each other. Then the woman stands up again and falls down, but in a different way. In a different position, with one arm under each leg. She looks like a knot. I'd have said she was epileptic or something, but no one thought of that. Maybe she didn't have an epileptic face; and she didn't really thrash or anything, just stood up and fell down again; they weren't normal convulsions. Anyway, stick with me: one of the passengers approaches and asks if she's okay, but she doesn't look around at him. Instead, she writhes in the narrow space between her seat and the one in front. Then she springs up and gives a sort of awkward jump, like a draggletail (I love the word *draggletail*. My grandma used to use it for everything)."

"Keep to the point. Tell it properly."

"What a hurry you're in! Well, the passenger who'd approached looks at her boggle-eyed; he goes a little closer and touches her shoulder."

"Is she on the floor when the passenger touches her?"

"Yes, but crouching by then. She's huddled between the two seats."

"And the bus is still moving?"

"That's right. But stop distracting me. I was telling you about the man, the one who touched her shoulder to see if he could help. It's like he's given the woman an electric shock. Just as soon as he touches her, she throws her arm back and hits a little girl's leg. By accident, apparently. The girl cries out. The man who tried to help the Woman Who Fell First, who people have dubbed the Good Samaritan, sinks to the floor, just like she did before him. Then he gets up and starts jumping. He's been infected."

"And what do all the other passengers do?"

"There aren't that many of them. Only four seats are occupied, in addition to the Good Samaritan and the Woman Who Fell First: the girl and her mother, a worker on his way home, a kindergarten teacher, and a teenager looking at his cell phone. And the driver, of course, but he hasn't noticed what's going on yet. Or he's pretending not to have noticed."

"So what happed next?"

"I'm getting there. It isn't an easy story to tell. I heard it from my brother; he witnessed the second part of it all. But I have to give you a few details."

"Like that one of the passengers is a kindergarten teacher?"

"Exactly. But I said all that because of the phone. The Teenager points his cell phone into the aisle and starts recording a video of the scene, or uploading it live onto the internet. You must have seen it: the Good Samaritan goes on jumping up and down in the middle of the bus, the Woman Who Fell First is moving very slowly, like a chick hatching from an egg; she looks unhinged."

"Yes, I watched the video, but I get it mixed up with others I saw from those days."

"I'll describe it all, then. The phone moves around a lot and the picture isn't very clear, but it seems that the Girl's Mother crosses herself and starts to pray under her breath. The Kindergarten Teacher cautiously approaches the Good Samaritan, walks past him, and squats down by the Woman Who Fell First. The Worker, who's in the very last seat of the bus, which has slowed down to ascend a steep street, hops off through the open rear door. The Woman Who Fell First makes another sudden movement and the Kindergarten Teacher backs off."

"I can picture it."

"The Good Samaritan starts jumping again, limp and twisted, awkward like, as though his rump's itching, and he's begun to shout too. Of course, by now the driver's realized that something odd is going on."

"And the Teenager?"

"He's still filming. But now it isn't a single, long video, but short, five- or ten-second clips he sends to his friends on WhatsApp."

"I've seen them."

"The whole world's seen them. Just think of it, they were on the news in China."

"Well, go on."

"You know the rest. You've heard it all before. You wanted to know how it started and I've told you."

"But didn't you say it started in a lot of places at the same time? What about the university?"

"What about it?"

"How did it start there?"

"I'm tired."

"In a psychology class, wasn't it?"

"I don't know where they got that from. It wasn't a class; it was in a corridor of the department."

"And . . . ?"

"It's kind of like what happened on the Ruta 3: a woman falls to the floor. Someone goes to her aid and soon seems to get infected and starts shaking like she's possessed by the devil as well. Everyone else looks on, stupefied. Nothing much more happened at the university. It soon fizzled out, no one else was infected. And nobody took a video, which is strange."

"I heard there was a video, but it was taken down from the internet."

"I don't think you can do that. But look, I'll go on telling you about the Ruta 3, the bit my brother saw: the driver stops the bus and asks everyone to get off. Particularly the Woman Who Fell First and the Good Samaritan, who are still moving (he's jumping and she's crawling). But they ignore him. The Girl starts crying, hiding her face in the Girl's Mother's lap. Her sister had disappeared a few weeks before. The Girl's Mother is worn out. She's spent days going from the police station to the Palacio Municipal, and the Military Zone 24 barracks. She and her younger daughter are on their way home after spending an hour in line at the public prosecutor's office, without even being seen. Up to then the Girl had held back her tears. And, afraid she'll start to cry herself, the Girl's Mother says to her daughter: It's just a game, we can jump up and down too. It's a desperate move, but this is a tale of desperate moves."

"And they begin to jump?"

"Yes, but the driver threatens to throw them all off. The Girl's Mother hurries the Girl off through the front door. And the Girl goes on jumping when they're on the sidewalk. She looks quite happy. The Good Samaritan gets off through the rear door and, once in the street, throws himself to the ground again, but this time he's injured because he slams onto flagstones. My brother says there was blood on the ground. The Woman Who Fell First hears the Good Samaritan cry out and disembarks too."

"And the Kindergarten Teacher?"

"The Kindergarten Teacher realizes the bus isn't going any farther on its route. Something extraordinary has happened and she can't figure it out. She gets off and stands watching the Good Samaritan, who's clutching his leg and has blood coming through a rip in his pants, around knee level. The Woman Who Fell First throws herself onto the flagstones too but isn't hurt. It seems she knows how to fall better than the man. The Girl's Mother and the Girl head off down the road, skipping and elbowing the walls as if they were made of rubber. Several passersby stop to see what's going on, and among them is my brother. Two women wearing aprons, standing in the doorway of a small shop, witness the scene from farther down the road, but they keep their distance."

"And the Teenager?"

"He gets off too. There are no passengers left on the bus now. The Ruta 3 continues up the hill a short way and then turns into a side street, where it only just fits. The driver is going home. No way is he even thinking of completing his route. He's been feeling unwell for days, and now this happens: his passengers throwing themselves onto the floor and screaming like lunatics. He's in no mood to finish his shift. He arrives home and sits at the table to wait. Two hours later his wife comes back and asks why he knocked off early, and he tells her that everyone on the bus started doing weird things. Then she tells him that she was coming from the market and saw strange things there too: people jumping around and shouting, and others moving very slowly, like they were on downers."

"But what about the Teenager? You were telling me about him."

"Oh, yes. The Teenager has gotten bored of the scene and can't be bothered to go on filming. He's laughing at the comments his friends post on the group chat where he sent the videos. They're making fun of faces the Woman Who Fell

First makes. They don't ask or care what is happening: the world's like that, they think; sometimes things happen that have never happened before. The Teenager puts his phone away and starts to walk home. He's alone, on a dirt track. Every so often he remembers what he saw on the bus and smiles to himself, or gives a little jump and twists his face a bit, as if he's imitating the Woman Who Fell First. He wonders what's happened to those people. If they're now jumping and shouting somewhere else in town. It suddenly occurs to him that his own behavior wasn't particularly smart. Maybe they really did need help. He could maybe have done something or asked if he could do something. Instead of filming what was going on, he could have used his phone to call an ambulance. But he doesn't know what number to ring for an ambulance or the police, he thinks. He doesn't know any number that isn't in his contacts. And anyway, the police are never the best option. They fucked up one of his cousin's eyes when they punched him for smoking pot in a gully near the trout farm. True, his cousin is a bit of a mobster, and he most probably yelled something at them, something abusive. But even so. That's no reason to beat him up so bad he ends up losing an eye. That's what's passing through the Teenager's mind. And as he's thinking that and walking home, he gets one more message from the group chat. From a high school friend. His friend says he was on his way to his mother's stall in the center when he saw some people doing things on the edge of the market. He's sent a video but it won't download. The Teenager tries several times without success; something has gone wrong. Then his credit runs out. That's what you get for sending videos from the bus. And the end of the month is a long way off. His dad gives him fifty pesos to top up his cell phone, in case of emergencies, but he always uses it up early."

"I heard a different story."

"Really? Tell me. I don't believe you can have a more first-hand version than mine, but let's hear it."

"I was told that the Kindergarten Teacher and the Teenager walked off together up the street. And they turned off into the forest instead of toward the church. And then went on walking in the forest, hand in hand, as though they'd known each other their whole lives. And they weren't just walking, but kind of skipping. Like two happy schoolchildren in Switzerland or somewhere like that. But the happy little skips start to change into bizarre leaps. Plus they're getting dangerously close to the fires. Sometimes she lifts one leg too high, loses her balance, and falls, but she gets up and moves on, still holding the Teenager's hand, her legs covered in bruises. And he sometimes shakes his head and shoulders, looking down at the ground, like he's trying to shake off an insect that's stinging his back. And then he walks on. I heard they went on like that for three days. There are people who say that by some miracle they managed to pass through the flames. Others claim they figured out where the fire was and took another Ruta, or that they came to a river and followed it, with water up to their waists. No one knows if they ate anything during that time, or if they at least sat down at night or slept on their feet, still jumping."

"To be honest, your version sounds a bit outlandish. But, whatever, you heard all sorts of things during those days. Who knows?"

"Yes, that's what I thought too. But it's reliable; it was in the newspaper. Supposedly the Kindergarten Teacher and the Teenager were seen on a path that runs through the ravine, walking aimlessly, falling down and yelling, snorting to get rid of the black ashy snot from their noses, turning their heads in circles until you'd think they'd break their necks. And they went on like that through the scorched undergrowth, bare trees, and dead squirrels. It isn't clear how they survived, but they continued on and someone saw them first thing in the morning of the third day, passed out on the bank of one of the Lagunas de Zempoala. He was a national park warden who'd gotten up early to collect the trash before the handful of tourists who were still visiting could turn up. He was sweeping the area where a man has a kite stand when he spotted them in the distance, beside the lake, lying half-naked, like a pile of rags. And they say the Warden rang his brother-in-law first because he's a police officer. And the brother-in-law said, 'Don't move them, they must be the ones that were kidnapped a few days ago.' But when the officer arrived, an hour later, he told his boss over the radio that it wasn't them; they were a couple of strangers, still alive, but like they were plastered. They thought they'd probably gotten drugged from inhaling so much smoke; they were covered in soot and their clothes were in tatters."

"And didn't it occur to anyone to think they had something to do with the mayhem in Cuernavaca?"

"At first, no, because the Teenager and the Kindergarten Teacher weren't moving; they weren't contorting themselves or doing any of that stuff they showed on the news. The Huitzilac police had been watching the whole thing in Cuernavaca on TV, but they thought it was just a made-up program, or someone exaggerating the truth. No way were people going to start doing that stuff for no good reason. But then the Teenager and the Kindergarten Teacher recovered. They'd been put in an ambulance and rehydrated, and there was talk of taking them to the health center to be checked over, when suddenly the Teenager made a strange noise, like mooing, and got out of the ambulance and began to shake his body like he was dancing reguetón, but harder. And the Kindergarten Teacher got out too and started moving her hips like she was having sex with the chilly breeze coming off the lagoon, with the mist hanging over the water, with the birdsong and the quad bikes in the distance, and the sound of the first ovens being fired to heat the comal for the tlacoyos."

"What happened after that? Why have you stopped?"

"I'm trying to remember. I get the stories mixed up. I don't know if I read this in the newspaper or someone told me . . . Oh, right. Then one of the police officers aimed his gun at them and told them to quit fooling and hand over the drugs. Because he thought they must have been smoking rock. But the Teenager and the Kindergarten Teacher took no notice. She went on making love to the sounds and the air, and the smoke clouding the sky, and he went on shaking his whole body, and then he ran to the Kindergarten Teacher, grabbed both her hands, and they twirled around like lovers, heading in the direction of the lagoon. And then there was a gunshot. The Teenager fell headfirst into the mud and the Kindergarten Teacher stood very still, as though she'd suddenly woken from a dream where she'd been forced to dress up as a cat."

"Did they kill him?"

"The Teenager? Of course they did. The police killed him

and then they put him back in the ambulance, taking advantage of it still being parked up there. They threw the Kindergarten Teacher into a patrol car and supposedly took her to the station to make a statement. But nothing's been heard of her since."

"That's the part of the story I can most easily believe."

"But what I do know is that those two are on the disappeareds list. Their faces were shown on a news bulletin, alongside the Good Samaritan and the Woman Who Fell First."

"I didn't know that. It's not the story I heard."

"What else were you told?"

"About the market."

"Which part? Was it when the fire broke out?"

"No. Some girl jumped up on a fruit stand and started kicking everything. People got really annoyed and the woman who owns the stand took a broom to her."

"And then?"

"Everything got in a muddle. A man who was coming up to buy something thought the woman was beating her daughter with the broom handle for the hell of it, and he protested. The Stand Owner began to explain it wasn't so, that the girl in the technical school uniform had jumped up on her stand without so much as a by-your-leave and had damaged her goods. But the Customer didn't believe her and when he turned to question the Technical School Girl, she was on the ground moving her hips in a weird way, like she was dancing lying down, and with her eyes bulging, fixed on some point on the market ceiling."

"I heard about the Technical School Girl too. But in my version, the Stand Owner didn't hit her on purpose, she just started waving the pole she used to take down the gourds and everyone thought she'd gone blind."

"Why blind?"

"Because she went off through the aisles waving the pole and knocking into things, as though she was blindfolded at a piñata party. They thought her husband had given her toloache, to get his own back. But then another of the traders said she was a widow, so they had no explanation for why she was acting the fool in the meat section. And that's where the whole thing really hotted up."

"What happened?"

"The Stand Owner threw a pig's head to the floor, she grabbed it by the snout and shook it, showering everything with blood. It splattered the skirt of a gringa who was taking photos and she almost had a dizzy fit. It was like carnival: there was pig's blood and streamers—nobody knew where they came from. And the gentleman who sells coconut water slipped in the pig's blood and injured himself. After that, the police turned up and threw them all into the street to carry on their outrages there."

"Incredible. I'd never have thought I'd live to see anything like it. And what seems to me most concerning of all is something two doctors said later on the radio, when they were commenting on the events: the infected people, the ones who were dancing, experienced some form of joy, an inexplicable jubilation, as if they'd managed to take off a filthy overcoat. Days afterward, some of them died of depression or overexertion, or because they wouldn't eat. Many more had minor injuries, lost a leg, or fell into a sort of lethargy that they still haven't overcome. But those who did recover, the ones who were able to break the absurd spell that had them shaking their bodies, and holding hands and going around in circles, all of them have permanent, sweet smiles on their faces thinking of the days, the weeks of carefree dance, the first dance plague since the Middle Ages, that sacred or damned event that took the lives of over four dozen Morelenses, that unplanned revolution that went nowhere but took ahold of girls and boys for two weeks."

I located Erre's parents, but they were unwilling to tell me much. They say their son disappeared before the kick dance and had nothing to do with it. They're afraid he's been kidnapped or that his body will turn up in some mass grave in ten years' time, with nobody knowing how it got there or why. They haven't reported him missing because it's said to be dangerous, and I guess that's true. I assume they are pulling strings or investigating on their own account, and their secrecy must, to some extent, be due to that.

But, for my part, I've managed to reconstruct the events through my own inquiries. Claudia, a former high school classmate I contacted via social media, told me she'd seen Erre and had a mezcal with him the day before Natalia's performance. She said Erre seemed to get drunk very quickly, but she didn't think it was anything worse than that: mezcal hits us all harder now we're past thirty.

That night, Erre didn't return to his parents' home but, according to one of the videos going around that document the events, two days later he was somehow mixed up in the Santa María episode: you only get a glimpse of him, standing, one hand touching his painful shoulder, staring in astonishment at a boy writhing on the ground. That's my only clue, but it's enough to tell me that Erre's parents have gotten it wrong: their son disappeared during the kick dance.

The obvious deduction is that he was on his way to see Natalia. He may well have found her home and gone with her to Tepoztlán, and Natalia didn't want to tell me because at times she can be mysterious and evasive, not to say an asshole. They may be living together in some shack in Amatlán de Quetzalcóatl, hiding out from Argoitia's fury, from the outbreak of dance and its repercussions. They probably think I'd be jealous if I found out they were loving up without me, that they'd excluded me from the amorous holy trinity that marked our adolescence.

But it's also possible—and this is a thought I find more frightening because it rings true—that Erre started dancing and was one of those rash souls who went up the flaming hillside and never came down. There's no way of knowing.

The highways have finally been reopened. A whole heap of Cuernavaca residents immediately took to the road for fear the dancing would start again or the smoke and looting return. But it's dawn now, and I don't think there will be much traffic.

Dad is packing a bag for the long-awaited trip to Acapulco

to say farewell to the sea—as we should have done before all this started. He's wearing the sky-blue guayabera he loaned me that day but it's kind of big on him: he's been losing weight lately. He's mostly lost interest in hearing the sea for the last time, but when I suggested the trip, he meekly acquiesced. I told him I was willing to drive the Chevy only if we set out at six in the morning to avoid the hordes of fleeing Morelenses.

During the outbreak, Dad sometimes listened to the radio. He used to tune into a local news station because he said the big nationals were just sensation seeking. But his favorite Morelos station didn't check its facts: it had a single journalist assigned to the job and the poor man was trudging the streets of the city, audio recorder in hand, interviewing a very diverse range of people: sociologists and juice vendors, doctors and housewives. The resulting mosaic of incompatible voices formed a grisly tableau of what was going on.

Magical explanations sprinkled with hard facts were given preference, but at times it was like listening to the commentary on a rugby game or an incomprehensible dithyramb about people being hunted with tranquilizing darts. Like a painting by Bosch described by someone who's taken magic mushrooms.

I spent the first days in a state of anomie, as though the scrap of the brain that determines and orchestrates emotional reactions had been surgically removed. Then I began seeking out friends, acquaintances, exes. I sent generic messages to all my contacts asking for reports, and received replies that ranged from memes to biblical commentary until I put all the conversations on hold and sought refuge in the solitude of marijuana. My dealer took full advantage of the situation, offering edible products capable of knocking you senseless for six hours. Those of us who value the subconscious enough to want to protect it from the news occasionally allowed ourselves to fall into the arms of narcosis.

Only the sounds of ambulances—hanging in the air like a warning—shook me out of my induced stupor from time to time, and when that happened I'd leave my bedroom and try to persuade my silly father to turn off the radio and share a bowl of pureed potatoes with habanero sauce (a dish of my own invention that I was proud of, and which my father bore with ill grace). He'd give way eventually and sit with me at the table, where we'd attempt to talk about something, anything, else. I'd ask him about the Tlatoque, who ruled the Tierra Caliente before the conquest; the obsidian brought from Xochicalco that was exchanged for feathers gathered in the southeast; the tunnels where the Red Bishop stashed weapons in the seventies; the aplomb with which Ivan Ilyich bore his cancer, without recourse to the pharmaceutical industry. And my father would respond to all my prompts with well-chewed anecdotes, spoken in a quiet tone, with no trace of his former fervor, almost robotically—a professor giving a lecture he knows by heart.

One evening, my mother called. Dad answered the phone in the living room, but as I was mooching around not far away, I was able to get close enough to hear the voice on the other end of the line. She told him she was in Minnesota, living in the suburbs with the ophthalmologist, and had seen the news, but didn't have any idea what was going on. She wanted to check we were still alive, nothing more, and as soon as Dad had confirmed that I was fine, she put down the phone without another word.

Sunup finds us on the outskirts of Chilpancingo: with a bloodied gauze of fine red cloud covering the skin of the sky. We stop at a gas station to buy potato chips and coffee and the assistant asks if we've come from Cuernavaca. Yes, I reply, but we didn't see anything. She glances at my father, who's using his stick to try to find the exit, and gives a loud, clear laugh. Have a good journey, she says, and don't bother coming back. That advice seems to me uncalled for, but I tell myself that the woman is half asleep.

Outside, Dad is leaning against the Chevy and he smiles when the wind strokes his face. He asks me to describe the scene before us. A barren high plain, dry dust, rocks, and wild dogs, I say. He gives a deep sigh and seems happy for the first time in ages.

Before we get back in the car, my phone rings. It's Natalia.

She tells me that Erre's body has been found, burned to a crisp. He was identified by his teeth, she says, and, like an idiot, I'm left wondering if I'd have recognized my friend's smile alone, without a body or any other context. Natalia goes on: Apparently, he was infected by the dance and started walking in the direction of Tres Marías; the investigators don't understand how he managed to make it to the very center of the wildfire without dying first. He was a stubborn beast, I tell Natalia, but she doesn't reply. We send each other love and promise to speak again soon, although we both suspect this will be the last time we'll hear the other's voice.

Dad, who heard it all, puts his stick and coffee on the hood of the Chevy and opens his arms to me. His jacket smells of mothballs and the hand he puts around the back of my neck is long and bony. I feel tears rising up from my gut, like the mercury in an old-fashioned thermometer, but they stick in my throat. While hugging my father, I think of Erre's smile when we used to run through the bamboo in the lot, when we were kids, and then I think of the black shirt he wore in those last days, of his pain and his permanently lost expression.

Dad squeezes my neck a little tighter. Still unable to cry, a lump in my throat, I stand there for a time, breathing. And then we leave.

Acknowledgments

It would have been impossible to write this book without the assistance of the Eccles Centre & Hay Festival Writer's Award (2020), which allowed me to work and carry out research in the British Library just before the outbreak of the COVID-19 pandemic.

I must also thank the Writer's Residence of the Latin American Art Museum of Buenos Aires, where I wrote part of the novel in the southern spring of 2019.

I would finally like to thank everyone at Editorial Anagrama; María Lynch, who read and commented on the manuscript; and Lilián Pineda, who taught me to dance.

DANIEL SALDAÑA PARÍS is a writer based in Mexico City. He is the author of the essay collection *Planes Flying over a Monster* and the novels *Among Strange Victims* and *Ramifications*.

CHRISTINA MACSWEENEY is an award-winning translator of Latin American literature. She has worked with such authors as Valeria Luiselli, Verónica Gerber Bicecci, Julián Herbert, and Jazmina Barrera.